God Forgives, The Streets Don't 2

By Blake Karrington

God Forgives, The Streets Don't 2

Copyright ©2013 Blake Karrington

All rights reserved

PUBLISHER'S NOTE:

This book is a work of fiction. Names, characters, businesses, organizations, places, events and incidents are the product of the author's imagination or are used fictionally. Any resemblance of actual persons, living or dead, events, or locales is entirely coincidental.

All rights reserved. No part of this book may be reproduced in any form without written permission from the publisher, except by a reviewer who may quote brief passages in a review to be printed in a newspaper or magazine.

Contents

Chapter 1	1
Chapter 2	7
Chapter 3	13
Chapter 4	22
Chapter 5	30
Chapter 6	39
Chapter 7	48
Chapter 8	58
Chapter 9	61
Chapter 10	69
Chapter 11	79
Chapter 12	87
Chapter 13	98
Chapter 14	107
Chapter 15	120
Chapter 16	129
Chapter 17	138
Chapter 18	148
Chapter 19	156

Chapter 1

"I've missed you like crazy, ma," Supreme stated sincerely into the receiver. "My time has been taken up with some really important business lately. So, now that everything is taken care of, we can begin right where we left off."

Silently savoring his sexy, northern voice, Monya couldn't help smiling. Plus, after the conversation she'd just had with Chez's supposed other woman, she was more than ready to experience some more of Supreme's good loving. Thinking of exactly how good his loving had been, she said, "Is that so?"

"Yes, it is," he replied, before quickly adding, "as a matter of fact, I need us to begin right now." He allowed a few seconds to lapse in order for his words to sink in. "Is it possible for you to get away and meet me at the same spot as last time, ma?"

Monya bit her lip as she anxiously tried to come up with a way to make the rendezvous with him possible. Although she knew that Chez would be home soon, after speaking with Neeta, she really didn't feel that he deserved her loyalty. "Uhh… yeah. I can do that," she replied. Fuck Chez! She screamed silently.

Supreme grinned as a sinister thought came to mind. *There is definitely no longer a reason for you to worry about finding a way to get around your man. It is a fact that a dead nigga can't stand in the way.* "That's great, ma! Call me when you arrive, alright?" Whether she knew it or not, it was just a matter of time before she would bend to his will.

"Alright," she passionately replied, thinking that this would prove to be her first step towards paying Chez back for his overwhelming acts of disloyalty towards her.

"Make it quick, ma. I need you bad, and I need you now!" Supreme demanded, ending their call.

Hearing the dial tone, Monya anxiously tapped her long nails against the huge marble and glass table, while she used her free hand to dial operator assistance. As she waited for the operator, she decided that after she received the hotel's number and made their reservations, she would pack an overnight bag and embark on the evening that she knew would be entirely too special.

Her body temperature rose at the thought alone. She needed to hurry up and make her exit before Chez arrived. With the way she was feeling, and the lack of attention she had been getting lately, she refused to allow anything or anyone to keep her from Supreme.

Exhaling, Dr. Daniels ran his pale white fingers through his sparse, slightly balding blond hair before staring down at the swollen, heavily bandaged patient lying in bed. "Well, we've done all that we can possibly do at this point," he stated matter-of-factly as he turned to face his colleague.

"You're right," Dr. Michaels replied, never taking her soft brown eyes away from the helpless patient who she had been staring at with a look that spoke of tender sadness. She sighed slightly and spoke in a low, somewhat emotional voice. "With the types of wounds he's suffered, he is extremely lucky to be with us this long. Now, I'm just hoping that what we did for him was enough to keep him alive, indefinitely."

"Whoever did this meant for our patient to be dead, Dr. Michaels. My time in the military showed me that when you place five .45-caliber slugs into someone, you mean serious business and death," Dr. Daniels remarked as he checked the many monitors that were connected to the critically wounded patient.

Shaking her head in disgust, Dr. Michaels continued. "You're saying exactly what I was thinking throughout the entire operation. It was far from an accident that one slug found its way into the chest and luckily missed his heart by a fraction of an inch, only to be followed by another that entered his back, coming close to his spine."

Massaging her temples, she added, "They barely missed his penis with the slug that tore through his thigh before nearly severing his elbow from the rest of his arm with another. He was truly blessed, because had the cheekbone not deflected the slug to his face, it would have surely ended his life. As you can see, the path it was traveling on would have definitely taken it through his brain on its way through the cranial wall." She shuddered at her last statement, and reached for the clipboard attached to the foot of his bed. "Right now, you have to be the luckiest man in the city," she whispered under her breath

"Well, there's nothing more we can do here," Dr. Daniels informed. "Come on. Let's go check on the rest of our patients, doc."

Dr. Michaels turned to follow her colleague out of the room. She suddenly halted her step and glanced back at the bed and the patient in it. With a look of despair, she mumbled, "God, if it is your will, I pray that you would watch over this one a little closer than normal for me."

She didn't really know why this particular patient meant more to her than the many others who had rested there before him. She figured that it more than likely came down to the fact that she was fed up with seeing her black brothers close to death and dying, due to senseless bullshit.

Exhaling, as if the weight of the world was suddenly upon her shoulders, she walked through the door and pulled it closed behind her.

Drugged up and unable to move, much less open my eyes, I laid in a sort of limbo state. Even unconscious, I was observant of my surroundings. That being the case, I heard every word that the doctors shared. I was fully aware that this shit was far from a dream, and I was really fucked up.

In a haze, the events that had led me to where I now found

myself were slowly beginning to return in bits and pieces. I had actually allowed myself to be caught out there, and the unmistakable accent of my northern assassin suddenly began to come back as well. Somehow, I was able to see the diamond encrusted gold that shined so brightly in his mouth as he stood tauntingly above me, with a look of hatred on his face, and the banger in his hand. It was too clear that my shooting had been in retaliation for the robberies we had committed.

I felt myself slipping into an even darker drowsy state as I thought of the last words I had heard the female doctor say before she left. Like her, I too hoped that God would watch over me a little harder than usual. I wasn't dead yet, so if he would give me a little extra attention, I would definitely lend a helping hand in staying alive. I wasn't ready to go just yet. Before I lay it down, I had to see ol' boy who did this to me one more time. He had to feel the pain I was now in. That was my only desire.

"Umm! You taste so-o-o good!" Monya hummed, greedily bobbing her head upon Supreme's protruding flesh.

Staring downward with clenched teeth and a look that dripped with lust, Supreme forcefully removed himself from her mouth as he leaned against the wall on unsteady legs and massaged the handful of curly hair that he held within his grasp.

Feeling the void of his exit, Monya looked up in alarm through eyes that were fogged with ecstasy. "Wh… what's wrong, baby? Did I do something wrong?" she stuttered, swallowing a mouthful of saliva.

"Hell nah!" Supreme boomed. His chest rose and fell rapidly as if he had just run a marathon. "The shit was feeling too damn good, ma. I just had to stop you so that I could allow the pressure to go down some." He glared at her through passion filled eyes as he found her hungry, wet squatting form entirely too irresistible to wait any longer.

With a light, unexpected tug of her hair, he pulled Monya up into a standing position.

She gasped at the intense, hungry look she witnessed in Supreme's eyes. Her chest rose and fell with her own excitement as she matched his stare through unblinking eyes and slightly parted lips.

He reached for a large red breast and greedily covered it with his mouth. Alternating between sucking, licking and gently biting the protruding, thick brown nipple, he massaged the underside of her other breast. Hearing her gasp for breath at his sweet assault, he placed two fingers inside of her tight, drenched opening and slowly rotated them against her satiny silk walls.

"Aww! " Monya moaned, pulling his head in closer against her breast and raising up on her tiptoes. She closed her eyes and rotated her middle to the exquisite feeling that was taking place within her center. Moving her ass in a slow, controlled motion, she bit her lip in surrender, and cried out, "Oh-h-h, Supreme!"

Supreme raised his head to peer at Monya's magnificent beauty. He worked his tongue into her parted mouth and began to duel with her rapidly swirling tongue. Noticing how her body was responding to his movements, he removed his fingers from inside her, and quickly grabbed both cheeks of her soft ass. Before she could anticipate his next move, he lifted her from the smooth tile in one swift motion and placed her directly on his hardness.

"Oh my God!" she screamed at the surprise invasion that felt as if it had split her center completely in half. "Supreme! Oh, Supreme!" she loudly moaned incoherently, raking her nails over his shoulders.

He held her still, allowing her time to accustom herself to his abrupt entrance. He winced at the mixture of pain from her stinging nails, and the extreme tightness of her center. Supreme ran his big hands over the smooth flesh of her soft ass. He suddenly felt the slight rocking motion of her body as it moved against his own. Placing his lips against hers, he slowly removed each inch from her greedily grasping tunnel, listening to the raspy gurgling sounds that slid from deep within her. Once at the tip of her opening, he purposely drove all eleven inches back inside her depths.

"Oh shit! Supreme!" Monya cried out, clawing at his back and shoulders.

She closed her eyes tightly at the fierce invasion. It was painful, but mixed with a touch of pleasure; she was unable to control the tears that cascaded down her cheeks as she felt the huge, piston-like piece of meat working her depths. Monya leanedback into the spray of the shower nozzle, arched her back, and began to ride the wave of ecstasy as she worked her middle with abandon.

On unsteady legs, Supreme repeatedly slammed himself into her. Her tightness was definitely something he could get used to.

"Fuck me! Supreme! Oh God, Supreme, fuck me!" Monya loudly ranted with an inferno of lust burning in her eyes.

She savored the sensation of something so huge impaling her, moaning and groaning to the top of her lungs as tears clouded her eyes. Yet, even in the throes of ecstasy, her heart ached for Chez and the life they once shared. It would never be the same again.

Feeling Monya's body trembling as her eyes rolled behind their lids, Supreme increased his strokes. Her inaudible cries proved to him that he had complete control of her body; her mind would soon follow. Although she wasn't aware of it just yet, she now belonged to him. Soon, the rest of his plan would fall into place as well… real soon.

Chapter 2

Sam was in heaven as he reclined in the Jacuzzi and watched his son's mother make love to the gorgeous female that she had brought home from the club the night before. This was a regular pastime for the two of them, and it served to enhance their relationship ten-fold. Nikki loved women just as much as Sam, and hunted for the most beautiful specimens that she could find, to share with her man.

He licked his lips at the scene that was taking place before him, delighting in the sweet moans that escaped the beautiful female's mouth as his girl devoured her. It never ceased to amaze him just how talented his girl was when it came to sexing another female. With her rapidly flicking tongue and expert fingers, she possessed the skills that drove bitches crazy.

The way that Nikki held eye contact with him as she kneeled between the trembling legs of the whimpering female caused Sam's erection to swell to painful proportions. Even after sexing the women numerous times throughout the night, not even his nearly exhausted state could keep him away from the pair as he eyed his girl's large ass.

As Sam stood and exited the swirling tub, dripping water all over the marble floor, he never relinquished eye contact with his woman. She was beautiful and he never tired of sexing her. His Puerto Rican goddess possessed the type of body that dreams were made of, and as he crawled behind her on the California King-sized bed, Sam couldn't wait to sample her goodies once more.

"What's good with you, playboy?" Qwen questioned, holding the phone between his ear and shoulder as he maneuvered the Porsche through traffic.

"You aren't going to believe this sucker shit when I tell you, man!" Pat replied with a laugh.

Pat was a money-getter from the Eastside of the City. He was quick to resort to gunplay when necessary, thus Qwen knew that whatever he was about to tell him was of the utmost importance.

"Talk to me, and let me be the judge of whether I believe you or not," Qwen said, prepared to receive Pat's news.

Exhaling, Pat said, "Look, where can you meet me? This isn't something that needs to be discussed over the airways."

"A'ight, I hear you. Meet me at Church's downtown. I'll be there in about fifteen minutes." Qwen ended the call and dialed Sam's number.

"Yeah Nikki, work that ass back for daddy!" Sam groaned as he stroked deeply into Nikki's depths. The harder he fucked her, the faster she flicked her tongue into the center of the female who lay shaking beneath her.

"Aaaahhh!" the female cried out as she wound Nikki's long hair around her fist and tried to force her face more firmly against her. She was nearly delirious with the pleasure that Nikki was giving her, and felt the stirring of another explosive tremor brewing within her center.

Nikki's moans were muffled due to her mouth being full, yet she too experienced a state of bliss as she enjoyed two of her greatest treats. Although she loved dick, nothing could compare to a hot, wet pussy. As she flicked her tongue in the female's wetness, while Sam stroked her insides, Nikki was in heaven.

Sam heard his phone ringing. His eyes traveled from the two women that moved beneath him to the phone that sat on the dresser. There was no way that he was going to stop what he was doing to answer it. As he felt Nikki's insides clamp down on him, any thoughts that Sam had about the phone or who was calling disappeared. His pleasure was all that mattered to him at that moment.

Pat's Cadillac was parked in the rear of the restaurant when Qwen pulled into the lot. He pulled up beside him and got out of the Porsche. Pat exited his car and extended his hand for a pound, then led Qwen around to the back of the Cadillac.

Pat looked around them nervously before sticking his key in the lock, then raised the trunk so that Qwen could view what was inside.

"Shit!" Qwen exclaimed loudly, stepping closer when the dead body came into view. He instantly recognized the face, even though it was swollen and bloody. Qwen stepped back and allowed Pat to shut the trunk. "Why is he in there?"

Shaking his head as he turned to face Qwen, Pat said, "The nigga came at me sideways, talking about you and Chez!"

Pat's words surprised Qwen. Him and Darryl were supposed to be cool. He would have never expected him to have any issues with Chez and himself.

"What did he have to say about us, man?" Qwen questioned, wondering what Darryl could have possibly said to make Pat kill him.

"Homie, he was speaking recklessly. Talking about Mann and some New York niggas that he was down with, and how they were gunning for you and Chez!" Pat spoke with a level of venom in his voice that showed his dislike for Mann and the New Yorkers. "You already know how I feel about out of town niggas, and I be dammed if I was about to side with them or anyone else against you and Chez!" It was clear that he meant every word of what he said.

"Yeah, I feel you on that babyboy... but what led to that?" Qwen asked, pointing to the trunk.

Pat laughed at the memory. "Darryl said that the New Yorkers were about to be the next big things in the city when you niggas were gone. He said that he was out recruiting a team of gun boys for them to assist in getting rid of you all. When I refused his offer and asked him to get out of my car, he didn't take it too well."

Chuckling at Pat's use of words to define the rage he was sure that Darryl had been in, Qwen stated, "Darryl always was a hot head."

"Yeah, he was. That's why I had to shoot him in it!" Pat stated angrily. "Would you believe that he had the nerve to call me a bitch ass nigga, because I wasn't willing to roll with them?"

"Yeah, I believe it… because I know how stupid he was," Qwen replied.

"Anyway, one thing led to another, and before I knew it, I had put one in his head and another in his chest."

"Damn, man. I hate that you had to catch a body behind some shit dealing with us. I appreciate your loyalty though, and know that Chez will feel the same when he hears about what you have done."

"The nigga had it coming, and I have no regrets with being the one who gave it to him. Plus, you know that you and Chez are my dudes." Pat said, waving the thanks off.

"No doubt!" Qwen exclaimed. "When you finally get that body out of your trunk, give us a call. Chez and I are going to do something for you."

"Sounds good to me," Pat said smiling. "Where is that nigga anyway? I tried to call him before I called you."

"I'm not quite sure," Qwen said, finding it odd that he hadn't spoken to Chez either. "Now that you mention it, I'm going to have to give him a call myself."

Dresser tossed his car keys on the night stand as he snatched up the remote control from the bed and headed towards the bathroom and the sound of running water on the other side of the door. Peeping inside, he caught a glimpse of Monica's naked, soapy frame through the fogged up partition, and lightly inhaled the Backwood cigar.

"I'm home, boo," he informed her.

"Huh? Oh! You startled me!" she smiled, sticking her head partially out of the shower. "You're just in time though," she added teasingly, exposing a tender brown, soapy breast and enough thigh to indicate what waited on the other side of the partition.

"Come on in and keep me company," she purred in a husky, seductive voice.

Reflecting on the menage a trois he had just experienced at the hands of two highly qualified college sophomores, Dresser blew out a gust of smoke and smiled inwardly. "Nah, baby. I'm too tired. I'm going to have to take you up on that offer later. Alright?" He winked his eye and backpedaled out the door before a response to her frown could reach his ears.

Back in the bedroom, he sat on the edge of the bed and kicked his shoes off as he surfed the vast array of channels on the 50-inch screen.

"Baby, bring me a towel!" Monica yelled, interrupting his nightly ritual.

Dresser cut his eyes in the direction of the bathroom and his features changed into a grimace. "How the fuck do you take a shower without a towel?" he disgustedly mumbled in a low tone, meant more for his ears than hers.

As he turned to handle the task, the blunt suddenly toppled from his parted lips. "What the hell!" he wailed at the sight that stood clearly before him on the television screen. In disbelief, he dropped down on the bed and openly gawked at the image of Chez's 840 Beamer surrounded by police cruisers and paramedics. In awe, his mouth hung open as he listened to the reporter with wide eyes and his heart beating out of his chest.

"We're at the scene of a double shooting that has left an unnamed female dead, and a local man in critical condition. The male has been identified as Sanchez Viles. We have learned that upon reaching the Medical College of Virginia, he was found to have suffered five gunshot wounds.

"After searching the vehicle that the victim was found in, the police surprisingly found two kilos of what appeared to be cocaine, and a .40-caliber handgun inside the trunk. The authorities plan to prosecute this case to the fullest extent of the law, if and when the suspect recuperates..."

"Damn!" Dresser whispered with a sour look plastered on his

features.

"Where the hell is my towel, nigga?" Monica questioned in a hateful tone, with her hands planted on her dripping wet, naked hips.

The look on Dresser's face changed her angry drawl into a softer, more sincere tone. "What's wrong, baby?" she asked. "You look like someone just died or something." She followed his eyes back to the television and instantly clutched her chest. "Oh, no!" she squealed, tightening her lips to control her emotions, but unable to stop the flow of tears. "Nooooo, Chez! Dresser, what's going on?"

Dresser opened his mouth to reply, but nothing would come. Just like Monica, he wanted to cry. The only difference was, his tears were hardly going to be for Chez, or anyone else for that matter. His only worries were for himself. If, by chance, Chez didn't make it, he would have to find a way to stay afloat without him. At this point, the last thing he planned to do was return to the broke, overlooked Dresser of the past. The game had changed, and so had he.

Dresser realized that it was all about him, and staying on top. So, whatever Chez's situation turned out to be, as long as Dresser still held five keys that belonged to him, he knew he would be just fine.

Chapter 3

The news of Chez's shooting had spread throughout the city like a wildfire, catching their crew by surprise. It was Qwen who took it the hardest, as he was closest to Chez. Then, to make matters worse, for the last week, it had been impossible to make any contact with Chez. The 24-hour police presence at the hospital, and their refusal to allow him any visits or phone calls, kept his loved ones away.

If that wasn't bad enough, after the shooting it seemed as if an invisible force had swept upon their business as well. Sales were moving at an all-time low. Qwen couldn't figure out just what was happening, but he planned to do so as soon as possible.

Ty's shipments were now almost non-existent, after purchasing no less than ten keys a week from them to supply the Eastside. He would be Qwen's first stop.

He glanced towards Sam, who seemed to be brooding over his own thoughts. "Hit the Eastside, yo. I have a feeling that Ty knows what's poppin."

Feeling the weight of his weapons as he leaned further into the passenger seat, Qwen hoped for Ty's sake, that he wasn't on some shady shit. If by chance, that was the case, the Eastside would have a replacement before the end of the day. Who his replacement would be, Qwen couldn't care less. What he did care about was the forty keys that sat in the stash house drawing dust. If he had to go on a murder spree to get them sold, a murder spree would be the remedy.

In the few weeks since my shooting, I had come through well. I was stapled, stitched, and bandaged all over, but through the grace of God; I was still alive. I was sure that after my close call, I had used up the last of my nine lives. Thus, I would have to make this one count. Looking down at my arm and the cuffs that held me captive, I realized that I wasn't quite out of harm's way just yet.

I exhaled disgustedly as I pondered the fact that after everything I had been through already, here I was, facing a gun and drug charge that looked like a no win situation. I shook my aching head, as the realism of the words 'when it rains it pours' came to mind. It was accompanied by the realization of truth, because at the moment, I definitely couldn't find a way out of this storm that I was caught in.

The way they were treating me here, with no phone or visits, I may as well have already been in prison. I needed to see my crew and put them up on game. I had a business to run, and more than anything, I needed to see my woman and child. The thought of Monya brought my shooter's words back to mind once more. *I'll take care of your bitch for you, nigga.* My mind was running rampant with the implication of him actually meaning her. Then, as quickly as I went there, I changed course. Monya would never do that to me, so he had to be speaking on a straggler.

"Yeah, that's what he meant," I mumbled through parched lips, more for my own benefit than anything else. Only, deep down in my soul, a part of me that couldn't be denied, recognized the possibility that Monya was exactly who he meant.

Clearing her throat as she walked into the room, Dr. Michaels smiled. "Hello Mr. Viles."

I savored the sweet scent of her perfume as I looked in her direction. It dawned on me that her smooth, chocolate complexion, wide hips and tiny mouth-full breasts were just what I was in need of to begin my day. A certified beauty in my book, her little Toni Braxton hairstyle and dark smoldering eyes only added to the already perfect package.

Smiling flirtatiously, I responded, "Hello, beautiful."

She bashfully averted her eyes from me to the clipboard she held, and blushed. "So how is my favorite patient doing today?"

"I'm feeling more and more like myself every day," I replied inwardly wincing at the pain I was trying hard to hide.

"That's great," she remarked, still staring down at the chart.

Grinning devilishly at the mischievous thoughts that were running rampant through my mind, I made a bold suggestion. "If you have a little time, I sure could use a quick sponge bath."

Dr. Michaels raised her eyes from the chart and stared at me for a moment. She then lifted her glasses and gave me an uneasy sigh, before finally revealing one of the sexiest dimpled smiles of all-time. "I... I don't think so, Mr. Viles." She innocently stuttered, then added in a jovial tone, "If I have to give you a sponge bath, it's definitely out of the question."

Erupting in laughter, my whole body hurt from the inside out as I spoke through an unsteady voice. "I'm only playing, doc. I can take you up on the sponge bath when I'm released."

"Umm-hmm," she replied, openly blushing. Staring back down at the chart, she cleared her throat. "Speaking of being released, I really came to inform you that I've signed the papers to have you placed in the custody of the authorities."

"What?" I questioned, confused. "Sign me out? How, doc? I'm still fucked up," I argued vigorously, in a voice that carried a troubled tone.

Sighing, she shook her head in despair. "It's out of my hands at this point. The jail you're being transferred to has an exemplary medical staff that can handle the rest of your care." With down cast eyes, Dr. Michaels spoke in a low tone that was barely above a whisper. "I wish you the best, Sanchez. I'm so sorry."

Frustrated, I dryly stated, "Me too, doc. Me too. When do I leave?" I questioned with a piercing look in her direction.

"Uh..." she hesitated. "You... uh, leave today."

Monya hated what had happened to Chez. Her first response was to run to him and forget every detail of her conversation with Neeta. However, upon hearing the account of the woman who was with him, then seeing her face, Monya's heart turned ice cold. Not only was the female rumored to have been wearing only a coat with no other clothing beneath it when she was killed; she was the same woman Monya had seen Chez cozying up to in the park months before. With that thought in mind, along with what Neeta had disclosed to her, and the knowledge of all the women who had come even before them, Monya was more than fed up.

Disgusted beyond belief with what Chez had so easily put her through over the years, she found it impossible not to smile at the new and beautiful side of her life. This side of her life was where she received the love and support that had been missing for entirely too long; the side that Supreme now occupied so unselfishly.

Smiling even harder, Monya found herself drifting into a dream state that she hadn't experienced in countless years. She sucked on her bottom lip as the thoughts flowed. She subconsciously relived every night that they had spent in each other's arms since Chez's shooting. Every single moment of their time together had been so special, and after being alone, Monya realized that she wasn't prepared to lose what they had found.

Going back to the life she lived prior to encountering Supreme wasn't an option. Therefore, she had thought long and hard before coming to a conclusion. After what had seemed like a lifetime with Chez, it was over. Not only did she long to begin living her own life, she longed for what had been absent for too long to recall. Happiness.

Missing Supreme and counting the moments until they would be together again, Monya decided that it was her turn to make Chez suffer the same way she had. Sighing uncomfortably, Monya hoped that she wouldn't have to regret her decision down the road. Whether she still loved Chez or not, as of right now she was with Supreme.

Supreme spoke to Ty through the lowered Range Rover window, while glancing through the rearview mirror at Tee, Unique, Shawn and Warren who sat in the black 560 Benz parked down the block. Refusing to take his security lightly since Rico's death, Supreme decided to bring a crew of his die hard soldiers down to assist him with his takeover.

"You got shit poppin' out here, son," Supreme stated flatly, scanning the busy block.

"Yeah, man. You... you know I got to stay up on my grind," Ty nervously responded. A phony smile was plastered on his face while his eyes remained locked on the Uzi sitting on Mann's lap.

"I feel that, money. But... ah, speaking of staying on your grind, I got ten more of those birds for you." Supreme fixed Ty with a cool, expressionless stare and added, "I'll send someone around to hit you off a little later, Alright?"

In a quivering voice as he looked around nervously, Ty replied, "I'm good right now, Supreme." He lowered his tone as he glanced from Mann back to Supreme. "I still have to finish the ones you sent me a few days ago before I cop something else."

"I see," Supreme scowled and glanced towards Mann, who lifted the Uzi and popped in the extended clip. Supreme slowly turned his head back to face Ty, and fixed him with an ice glare, before coldly stating, "Like I said, I'll have someone roll through and hit you off with another ten joints later. Have half my dough when they arrive, and you can make up the remainder on the next purchase. You got me?"

"Alright, Supreme," Ty mumbled with fear embedded in his voice and nervous eyes.

Ty wanted to object, but was afraid of the consequences he knew would follow. He noticed that Mann's attention was riveted behind him. He turned to see what it was that Mann was pointing out to Supreme, and his heart dropped at the sight of the approaching vehicle. Realizing that what he feared the most was about to pop off, Ty wished he would have never gotten involved with either group.

Supreme had a smug grin plastered on his face as he grabbed his phone and quickly punched in numbers. "Heads up, son. We've got intruders in the burgundy Beemer." He pulled a chrome nine from his waist and released the safety as he watched the 735 approach while speaking into the receiver. "Stay back, but be prepared to set it off if shit goes down."

Supreme ended the call and awaited the inevitable showdown.

Sam's face twisted up in a look of pure hatred, and he interrupted the light conversation between him and Qwen. "Brah, ain't that Ty standing over there kicking it with them niggas in the Range?" He recognized the truck from months before in the park. His adrenaline immediately began to pump at a dangerous level.

Catching sight of him as well, Qwen silently took in the scene as he reached for his twin four-fifths concealed in the small of his back. He also recalled the truck from months before, when Chez had knocked Mann out. Already having a suspicion that the niggas inside the Range or one of their people had played a part in Chez's shooting, Qwen was more than ready to give them a taste of vengeance.

"Yo, pull over there and we can close the distance between us and the truck on foot."

There was no need for any more words as Qwen excitedly prepared himself for the payback that had been gnawing at him since he found out about Chez's attack.

Keeping his eyes on the enemy, Sam made a mental note to personally murder Ty along with the scum inside the truck. Though Ty had been cool up to this point, if he wanted to deal with the enemy, he too was an enemy in Sam's book. He whipped into a parking spot that would allow them an easy escape route, once their work was done. Sam grabbed two nines from his stash spot, along with extra clips in case he had time to fill their bodies with lead twice.

Seeing the fear that was written all over Ty's face, Supreme wanted to explode in laughter. Like Ty, he too was aware of the move Qwen and Sam were in the midst of bringing them. Unlike Ty, he was prepared. They weren't aware of the trap they were about to run into, and little did they know, they were now breathing the last air their lungs would hold.

"Cuz, they're out the car and running in a low crouch, "Mann informed, cracking his door slightly as he raised the Uzi in preparation of the coming battle.

"Roll out, Ty," Supreme snapped. "Shit is about to get real nasty around here in a minute, and I wouldn't want you to catch a stray one," he said in a mocking tone, chuckling at Ty's speedy exit. Grinning at his cousin, Supreme grabbed his phone and hit redial. "'They just ran past your position. Set it off, money."

As Sam and Qwen jogged towards the target with their guns crisscrossed behind their backs, Qwen realized that something wasn't quite right when he noticed the passenger door crack open. The real alarm set off for him when he saw Ty running in the opposite direction, as if he feared for his life.

Halfway there, it was too late to change their course. The look Qwen saw in Sam's eyes when he glanced in his direction silently spoke more to him than any words Sam could have spoken from his lips.

Simultaneously removing their guns from behind their backs and raising them as they ran across the grass and entered the street, no words were necessary. There would be no turning back. Regardless of what happened in the next few moments, in their hearts, they each knew that the surprise they had planned, was now against them. They exchanged glances of solidarity as the rapid automatic gunfire erupted.

"It's on," Unique said, ending the call and popping the clip inside the Chinese made AK 47.

He narrowed his eyes at the two unsuspecting gunmen, who were making their way past the Benz in a low crouch. Unique smiled at the thought of how stupid they were as the sounds of other assault rifles could be heard all around him.

Unable to see into the interior of the Benz, due to the dark black tint, Qwen and Sam crept in front of it and slid into the street. He watched the gunmen step in front of the Mercedes and stare questioningly at each other. Unique held his breath. Whatever the reason for their hesitation, he silently prayed that they didn't somehow sense the danger and remove themselves from the trap they had carelessly walked into. Unique watched them remove their weapons from behind their backs before giving each other looks that said, 'Let's do it'.

As they raised their guns and moved forward, Unique removed the safety from his own weapon and gave the order

"Murder them niggas!"

The passengers opened their doors slowly, and slid out of the car with their weapons of death trained on the two unsuspecting gunmen. And then they opened fire.

Caught off guard, neither Qwen nor Sam knew how they had gone from the hunters to the hunted. No longer caring about the Range Rover and men inside, they both swung their weapons in the direction of the thunderous AK fire and cut loose.

Realizing that they were outgunned with nowhere to hide, Sam decided that he wasn't about to go without taking someone with him.

"Take this," he screamed, walking into the barrage of slugs with his own weapons spitting fire.

"Sam!" Qwen yelled loudly at the sight of his partner's head exploding before his eyes. "Nooooo," he shouted with pure hatred in his voice and fire blazing from his eyes.

He ran forward with no regard left for his own life, and fired into the group of AK toting assassins. Qwen saw two of them go down.

Still firing, he saw the surprised looks on the faces of their accomplices, and then he felt a slug tear into his stomach right before another embedded itself in his chest, causing him to do a summersault through the air. He landed on his face, and incredulously watched his weapons lying in the street, beyond his grasp.

Gritting his teeth in an attempt to block out the intense pain, he defiantly struggled to reach the closer of the two forty-fives, leaving a trail of blood behind as he crawled.

Qwen heard the sound of footsteps approaching. "You can do it," he whispered through clenched teeth.

He reached out to grab the gun, and sighed in defeat as a foot kicked the weapon further out of his reach. Staring upwards with the last of his steadily evaporating strength, he came face to face with one of the last people he wanted to exit the world at the hands of; Mann.

"Well, well," Mann laughed in a half-excited, half-hysterical manner, before kicking the already dying Qwen in the mouth. "Look what we've got here," he pointed towards his archenemy.

He tried to speak, but choked on the blood that fought to exit his open mouth, due to his injuries. Qwen knew that his time had arrived. Wishing that he could stay longer, he refused to go out like a punk. With that thought in mind, along with the reflection of the two men he had taken down on the way out, Qwen gathered all his remaining strength and spit a glob of blood on Mann's Timberland boots. He glared at the fury etched across Mann's face, through steadily darkening eyes. Qwen winked and fixed him with an evil smile.

Mann stared down at his boots in disbelief, squinted his eyes at Qwen and roared, "Smile at this, bitch!" He gripped the Uzi's trigger and sprayed the clip into Qwen's face and upper torso.

Supreme grabbed his cousin's arm to calm his rage, and commanded, "That's enough, Mann. He can't get any deader than he already is." Staring down at the faceless corpse, Supreme involuntarily shook his head. "Let's wrap it up everyone."

He turned to walk away, knowing that only one more man stood in the way of him owning the city. Now, the only thought he had was, *Where the hell is Boo-Boo?*

Chapter 4

Boo-Boo dealt with Qwen, Dresser and Sam, but without Chez in the picture, the relationship that he shared with the others just wasn't the same. Though he would have gladly gone to war for any of his friends, it was Chez that he felt the closest bond with. The two of them had been through a number of deadly situations together, and the loyalty that he felt towards Chez had been returned so many times. Thus, Boo-Boo took the assassination attempt on Chez's life really hard, and it had been eating at him for weeks. He had patiently played the waiting game, hoping for any word from Chez as to how he should proceed. No word had come, and Boo-Boo's patience quickly began to wear thin.

As he gathered his weapons and passed the blunt to his childhood friend, Vincent, Boo-Boo prepared to leave the project apartment that he had been stuck in ever since the news of his best friend's shooting had reached him. Never one to be afraid, Boo-Boo prided himself on his ability to out-think the next man. Therefore, since he wasn't sure who was responsible for Chez's attempted murder or whether he had been slated for the same predicament, he left Petersburg and headed back to Richmond and the projects that he had been raised in. If nothing else, Mosby Court would allow him a safe place to get his bearings. He had also been able to increase his riches while he laid low, because of the large amounts of money that flowed through the hood on a daily basis.

Watching Boo-Boo pack numerous weapons and ammunition into a large bag, Vincent exhaled a stream of weed smoke and said,

"You know that I will go with you, brah. Shit, all you got to do is say the word, and we can have an army of niggas ready to head down the Burg within an hour."

"Nah, I'm straight," Boo-Boo stated, never looking up from his task. "You know that I do my best work solo, playboy. I appreciate you though."

"Yeah, a'ight!" Vincent said, inhaling another gust of smoke.

As Boo-Boo lifted the heavy bag over his shoulders and gave Vincent a pound, he knew that he was mad at him. Even though he understood that his Richmond homies would have gladly come along to assist him with the caper, it wasn't what he wanted. If he needed help, Boo-Boo knew that Qwen, Sam and a number of Third Ward soldiers would hold him down. However, this was something that he needed to do alone. He was quite sure that the targets he sought were the ones responsible for what had happened to Chez, and blood was the only thing that would cure the heartache he felt. The last thing that Boo-Boo planned to do was share his healing process with anyone else. Everyone who died before the end of the day, would be by his hand and no one else's.

"Has anyone heard any news on the whereabouts of that nigga, Boo-Boo?" Supreme questioned, staring around the room filled with his New York and Fifth Ward soldiers.

"Cuz, none of our people have seen him or heard shit about him," Mann said, then added, "I even raised the reward another ten grand, and we still haven't had any luck."

Taking a sip from the Hennessey bottle that he held, Supreme thought about what he had just been told. "What's the chances that maybe he heard what happened to his crew and took off?" Although he doubted that was the case, he had tossed the scenario out there to see what type of feedback his people would give him on the subject.

Dax's laugh echoed through the large room, while a number of Fifth Ward soldiers either smiled or shook their heads. Mann spoke for the group. "Nah, Preme, you can forget that thought, Cuz. Even though I hate that nigga, I can still vouch for the fact that he's too damn crazy to be scared. He's still here, and he's sitting back waiting for the chance to put his murder game down. Let's just say that we need to find him before he finds us!" Mann laughed at the completion of his statement, but there was no humor in his laughter as it resonated through the room.

"I see," Supreme said, hearing the eerie undertone in his cousin's words. The last thing that he planned to do was allow Boo-Boo to catch him slipping, and there was no way that his scheme to takeover Chez's operation in the city would work until he got rid of him.

"Put a hundred grand on his head, Mann. I want all of you to keep your eyes open, and have your people do the same, just in case Boo-Boo is planning to do some renegade shit. Now, let's get back to getting this paper!"

As Supreme watched the men exit the room, wearing smiles and otherwise careless looks, he wondered if they realized how serious things were. Unlike the men around him, he saw the potential to create a dynasty in the city that most of his soldiers had grown up in, and had taken completely for granted. Boo-Boo was the last obstacle that stood in his way, and there was no way that Supreme would allow him to spoil his dreams of controlling the city and every hustler within it.

"Damn, Youngblood! I thought that you already knew about what happened to Qwen and Sam, man." Gator shook his head disgustedly as he averted his eyes away from the watery ones that held him with disbelief.

"How the fuck did they allow…" Boo-Boo began, before cradling his face in his palms and leaning up against the dirty wall of the vacant house.

After allowing the silence to engulf them for a few moments, Gator said, "I'm sorry to be the one to bring you the bad news, Youngblood."

He had lost enough of his own partners through the years to know how Boo-Boo must have felt at that moment. Yet, if Boo-Boo hadn't been aware of his partners' deaths, then Gator knew that there was no way that he could have known of the large reward that the New Yorkers had put up for any information that led to his capture. Because Gator liked him, not only was he not going to collect the reward money himself, but he was going to put Boo-Boo up on game so that none of the grimy dudes that populated the 3rd Ward would be able to collect it either.

"Look, youngin'. That isn't all of the bad news that I have to tell you…" Gator began, taking a step back and swallowing the saliva that pooled in his mouth when Boo-Boo turned to him with an evil look on his face.

"What else can you possibly have to tell me?" Boo-Boo spat. "Let me hear it! Come on, spit that shit out!"

Gator knew that Boo-Boo was hurting, and meant him no harm. Yet, because he also knew that he was a livewire, he decided to tread lightly. "You have always treated me fairly, youngster… and I dig you, so I feel that it's only right that I put you up on game. The New Yorkers that Mann and them deal with have placed a hundred grand reward on your head."

Boo-Boo laughed crazily. "Do you know where any of their dope spots are, Gator? If you can lead me to them, I will gladly give you the same hundred gee's that they are offering for my capture?"

Gator's face lit up like he had hit the lottery, as he began to calculate all of the things that one hundred thousand dollars could purchase him. "Yeah, I know where one of their dope spots is, youngblood."

"Let's go then," Boo-Boo spat, pushing the flimsy door aside that lead outside.

As he hurried towards the tinted Bonneville, the only thought that resonated in his mind was revenge. Where his enemies offered a measly hundred grand for him, he would gladly pay a million dollars to see that they suffered for what they had done to his friends.

Ice took his position as one of the organizations top lieutenants very seriously. After having to fight, steal, and at times kill for everything that he had ever obtained in life, the last thing that he would allow, was for anyone to take his newfound power from him. Thus, when he sped up in front of his dope spot and exited his newly purchased Toyota Supra, he carried a bag filled with heroin in one hand and a fully automatic Mac-11 in the other. He was a young murderer, and everyone who worked under him knew it. As he strode up the walkway, the many customers who stood in the long line stepped aside to let him pass.

"Move the fuck back!" one of Ice's workers who stood nearby wielding an aluminum bat barked loudly. "You see the boss coming through," he added, respectfully nodding his head at Ice as he passed and walked through the front door.

Ice's facial features never changed as he moved past his security checkpoints, and ascended the many stairs that would take him to the third floor trap spot. He had found the large three-story house and outfitted it in the manner that it was now in after witnessing the same set-up years before while in Baltimore. The way that Ice had set his dope spot up, it was virtually impossible for the police or stickup boys to penetrate far enough into its center to get near the dope or money. Too much security and too many guns stood between the front door and the jack-pot, and that was exactly how Ice wanted it.

"That's where they move their Helter-Skelter dope from, Youngblood," Gator stated, picking at a spot on his already pock-marked face.

Boo-Boo nodded his head, choosing to keep his response and thoughts to himself for the moment. He was surprised to see how many people stood in line to enter the huge, old house. From where they sat, he was able to count six big men who patrolled the orderly line with bats in their hands. Although Boo-Boo wasn't able to see any guns on the men, he realized that it was impossible for them to run such a large operation with nothing more than bats. He was sure that there were many gunmen inside, and Boo-Boo understood that there was no way that he would be able to attack them alone.

"Unless you have a death wish, Youngblood, I wouldn't suggest that you try them alone!" Gator sighed. He could see the chances of him ever seeing the hundred grand that Boo-Boo had promised him for the information, quickly dwindling.

"Yeah, you may be right, ole head," Boo-Boo agreed, thinking that Gator had pretty much read his mind. He needed to take the time to work out a much better plan of attack that would increase his chances for survival.

Boo-Boo placed the car in drive, and was about to press down on the accelerator when he saw something that caused his heart to race excitedly. "Muthafucka!" he smiled brightly.

"What, youngster?" Gator jumped, then stared at Boo-Boo wide-eyed.

Boo-Boo ignored Gator as he reached in the back floorboard and grabbed a bag. He stared off in the distance as he hurriedly removed banded stacks from the bag, and handed them to Gator.

"I owe you, but that's fifty stacks, O.G. I got you, but right now you got to get out!" Boo-Boo snapped, leaning over Gator and opening the passenger door.

Gator didn't know what had gotten into Boo-Boo to bring about such an instant change in him, but as he exited the car with the many stacks of money that now weighed his pockets down, he didn't care. As he turned and began to walk towards the house that held the ingredients that all his dreams were made of, the mysterious piece of the puzzle fell into place for him when he laid eyes on Ice as he got in his car and pulled off.

When the car that he had just exited sped past him, Gator knew that death wasn't far behind. As he took his place in the long line, he hoped that Boo-Boo survived the encounter with Ice. Gator liked him a lot, and if Boo-Boo didn't make it, there was no way that he would be able to collect his other fifty grand.

Although Ice had a number of individuals who he could have delegated the responsibility of making the drop offs to his spot, there were times that he liked to do them himself. He liked to make surprise appearances at his trap house. Though the threat of him popping up at any moment kept his workers on their toes, being more involved in the daily workings of his operations also kept Ice on point.

He whipped the Supra in and out of traffic, pressing the accelerator more firmly when he merged onto the highway entrance ramp. With darkness falling over the horizon, and nothing but the open road before him, Ice inwardly grinned as he shifted gears, allowing the sports car to reach speeds in excess of 100 miles per hour. Although he was aware that he should be more careful because of the Uzi and large amount of money that he carried inside the vehicle, the excitement that he felt overrode any caution that he would have normally exercised. Because of the life that he lived each and every day, and its serious and dangerous nature, Ice had only chosen that moment to enjoy his toy. Therefore, he saw no threat or alarm when the black Bonneville's silhouette raced past him. However, he saw a challenge when he witnessed the money that the driver carelessly tossed out of the sunroof.

Ice laughed loudly at the fact that whoever drove the souped up Bonneville was either stupid, or arrogant as hell. When one of the hundred dollar bills landed on the Supra's windshield, Ice said, "Okay, nigga! Let's see just how fast that old shit is fo'real," as he shifted into six gear and stomped the pedal.

"I got your ass now!" Boo-Boo spat as he peered through his rearview mirror at the fast approaching vehicle.

Ice had fallen for his ploy, just as Boo-Boo knew he would. He pressed the button to let the window down, and grabbed the Mac-90 machine pistol off the passenger seat. Boo-Boo saw that they seemed to be the only cars on the long stretch of highway. For as far as his eyes could see, they were alone. This would assist him in what he had planned.

When the Supra sped up beside him, Boo-Boo's heartbeat also sped up. He wanted to kill Ice so bad, that his vision was blurry and his hand shook as he raised the Mac-90 into firing position. When he realized that he and Ice were directly beside each other, Boo-Boo slowly peered sideways. He and Ice locked eyes, and in that exact moment, Boo-Boo compressed the trigger and sent bullet after bullet crashing through the Supra's windows and door.

Boo-Boo wasn't sure whether Ice had been hit or not, but as he peered through his rearview mirror, he saw the Supra smack into the concrete divider wall and flip over a number of times before coming to a stop upside down. Boo-Boo quickly placed the car in reverse, and backed up. He stopped a few feet from the crushed and smoking wreckage.

He exited the Bonneville with his weapon in hand. Boo-Boo proceeded with caution, just in case Ice was still alive. When he peeped inside the vehicle, he found that Ice's body was twisted and broken, just like the car. Though the two men exchanged unblinking stares, only Boo-Boo's eyes held life.

He stood and headed back to his own car. As Boo-Boo pulled off, he felt no remorse for Ice. He had only been a pawn in the game, and although Boo-Boo had no problem with taking out the low men who populated the New Yorker's organization, he wasn't going to stop until he got the king. The New Yorker had either killed or harmed everyone in his crew, and until he repaid him and his people for their deeds, he wasn't going to rest.

Chapter 5

The loud insistent sound of the ringing phone reverberated throughout the house.

"Baby, grab the phone! I know you hear it ringing," Monica yelled, fanning her hands in the air in an attempt to dry her freshly done nails.

Dresser frowned in irritation, and mumbled an inaudible reply under his breath as he headed in the direction of the phone.

Monica watched him as he made his way to the phone, and rolled her eyes. What she really wanted to do was scream, because the last few weeks had been hell with Dresser constantly stuck under her. Since the chain of events that had begun with Chez's shooting, she had noticed a fearfulness in her man that hadn't been evident in a long time. With his refusal to leave the confines of their home, getting her usual creep on had proved to be literally impossible.

"What?" he snapped when he picked up the phone. Hearing no response, Dresser was about to hang up when he heard the words that made his heart skip a beat.

"You have a collect call from, Chez. Will you accept the charges?" the operator questioned.

Dresser replaced the receiver and turned the ringer off with shaking hands. Nervous, but aware that he had already taken the first step in his plan to sever whatever ties remained between himself and his childhood friend. He was snapped out of his thoughts at the sound of Monica's loud outburst.

"Who the hell was on the phone?" Popping her lips loudly, she spoke with much attitude. "Damn nigga! You deaf or what?"

"It... it was nobody," he stammered.

Dresser was too deep in his thoughts of what needed to be done, to feed into an argument with Monica. He pulled a slip of paper from his pocket and strolled out of the room so he could make his next call in private.

After dialing the number, Dresser found himself trembling as he listened to the ringing phone. Unconsciously counting the rings, he was contemplating scrapping his plan and hanging up when the phone was answered.

"Yeah, what's up?" a voice boomed through the receiver.

Dresser cleared his throat, then spoke in a cracking voice. "Uh...I need...need to speak to Mann."

"You're talking to him. Now, how about you start by letting me know who the hell you are," he advised in a matter of fact tone.

Past the point of no return, Dresser took a deep breath. If he wanted to stay alive, and keep living large and in charge like he had become accustomed, this was the only way to do so. "Yo, Mann, this is Dresser. We need to talk. I'm looking for a position on a winning team." Gaining confidence, Dresser spoke in a firm tone. "You niggas seem to be holding the strongest cards in the city, so what do I need to do in order to get down with the squad?"

Mann removed the phone from his ear and smiled brightly as he stared at it in disbelief. He cut his eyes at Dax before he spoke into the receiver. "I think we may have room for you on the team after all, player. Now let's set up the meeting and rules."

I knew I wasn't trippin'. Dresser had just answered the phone and hung up on me. I wasn't quite sure what the hell was going on, but I found it hard to understand how someone could answer, hang up, and then allow the phone to ring continuously the next few times that I attempted to call back. I needed answers to my questions about Qwen and Sam's deaths, Monya's apparent disappearance, and the reason why I couldn't contact Dresser at the time when these answers were necessary. Therefore, the anger I felt as I dialed my home for what seemed like the millionth time since I had arrived at the jail, was warranted.

Seeing red as I listened to the ringing phone, the only thing that wore on my thoughts was revenge for myself and the deaths of my friends.

"What?" the male voice coolly questioned before the recording began.

"You have a collect call from, Chez," was the only thing I heard before I snapped to attention at the instant alarm that went off in my brain. My heart rate skyrocketed at the sound of another man answering my phone.

"Yo, Chez, what's up, son?" Supreme inquired in a mocking tone, with a hint of sarcasm.

"What's up?" I yelled. "Motherfucker who are you to be answering my shit in the first place?" I questioned in a rage, as I strained to determine if the moan I had just heard was a figment of my imagination.

"Hold on, son," Supreme instructed with a nonchalant chuckle. "It's for you, mama."

"Mama? What the fuck is going on?" I thought aloud as my heart threatened to beat straight out of my chest.

"Hello," Monya half spoke, but mostly groaned into the receiver.

"Bitch, who the fuck is up in my house?" I exploded. "Have you lost your fucking mind?" I added in a murderous rage, not even caring who heard my tirade.

"Listen to me..." Monya began.

"Listen to what, whore? You ain't saying shit!" I spat as my mind formed the picture of just what the hell was going on. "Monya, you know that I'm gonna kill you and that nigga, don't you?" I spoke in a low threatening tone.

"Huh?" Monya squealed. "Chez, hear me out," she cried out in a state of fear. "It's not what you think." Rambling, she stammered, "I... I'll... I will always love... love you, baby. I... I just need...to do me. Chez, please understand, I... I just want to be happy."

"Happy, huh? You just want to be happy. Ain't that some shit?" I said, laughing in a deranged manner. "Bitch, you will never be happy again after I get out of here! I'm gonna take my time and murder your funky ass nice and slowly, the way you deserve. And you know what --"

"Yo, son," Supreme returned to the phone, cutting my words short. "Respect the game. She chose me, and you ain't murdering shit. Check it though, so you'll know. I will gladly take care of your bitch for you. My bad, I forgot I already told you that shit the last time we bumped heads."

"Monya!" I shouted into the empty phone, only to hear her loud moans and passionate pleas for my archenemy to continue fucking her.

Dumbfounded, I didn't know what to say, or do for that matter. For the first time in as long as I could remember, I was truly helpless. I just placed the phone back on the hook in an attempt to maintain what little dignity I had left.

With murder in my mind, and hatred in my heart, I made up my mind that I would contact Neeta and reveal to her that a rainy day stash was stowed away in her house just for times like this. I would have her accelerate my release. After my lawyer was paid, and a bond was set, the streets would run red with the blood of my enemies. Monya now held that title as well, and regardless of how much she had meant to me throughout the years, she now had to suffer the same fate as the rest.

My hands shook as I raised the receiver once again, and pressed Neeta's number. I tried with all the strength left inside me to contain my rage. Calming myself as much as possible, I hardly heard the ringing phone as the pictures of Monya and the man who had tried to murder me, invaded my thoughts.

"Hello," Neeta purred in her too sexy voice.

"Hey, boo," I replied in a somewhat hoarse, cracked tone.

"Baby!" she screamed, "I've missed you soooo much. Are you alright? When can I come see you? I love you. Oh, my, God, who did this to you?" she rambled along in a questioning manner.

"Neeta, I need you to listen," I instructed, far from being in the mood to deal with her tirade. "Now, do I have your full attention, ma?"

"Umm hmm. I'm listening," she quickly retorted.

"Okay, this is what I need, so you have to follow this shit to a tee," I stressed before continuing. "In the garage, you will find a safe hidden in the ceiling above the skylight. Inside is over 380 grand. The combination is 12-21-11. Do you remember those numbers, ma?"

"I sure do," she replied.

"Alright. Once you open the safe, take out fifty grand and contact my lawyer, Benjamin Stevens. After he receives the retainer, he will handle the rest from there."

"I got you, baby," Neeta hurriedly butted in. "Don't worry about a thing, mama will handle your business," she proudly added.

Receiving a funny feeling in my gut, I reiterated my words, so that she would understand the seriousness of my predicament. "Neeta, I need you to take care of this immediately. I'm placing all my trust in you, baby. Do not let me down," I stated in a matter of fact tone that made it clear that her failure to accomplish my task wouldn't be acceptable.

"Yeah, I know," she replied with a tinge of irritation. "I got you, boo. Well, I'm gonna go get the money together and handle it now, Chez."

"Cool. Go ahead and get on it. I'll give you a call later, to see what he had to say, ma. And, Neeta, remember, don't let me down," I emphasized as I hung up and headed back to my cell.

"Yes!" Neeta screamed, dropping the cordless phone on the floor. "I'm rich!" she yelled over and over in a sing-song voice. "I'm fucking rich!"

Running through the house, she stumbled then stopped just long enough to kick her heels off before continuing on her route to the garage.

Reaching her destination, she rushed to the far wall and half dragged, half carried the wooden ladder to its desired spot. She broke a nail in the process, but Neeta paid no attention to it as she scurried up the stepladder and uncovered the section that Chez had advised.

Neeta found the safe exactly where he said it would be. She wasted no time flipping the dials; two times to the left 12, twice to the right 21, then once back to the left 11. Upon hearing the safe click, Neeta found herself hesitating as her heart rate increased drastically at the thought of so much money awaiting her on the other side of the door.

Exhaling deeply, she said, "Go ahead, bitch... get your money," while she pulled down on the latch, allowing the door to swing open on its own accord. "Oh shit!" Neeta mumbled at her first glance of the neatly banded stacks of crisp bills.

She felt her knees trembling and reached for the ladder to steady herself as she stared in amazement at more money than she had ever seen in her life.

She fingered the stacks; her eyes narrowed into greedy little slits as her mind worked overtime, devising plans on how she would enhance her style of living with her newfound riches. The fact that the safe and the money inside belonged to Chez was the furthest, most unimportant thought in Neeta's mind.

"Fuck him," she loudly stated.

There would be no fifty grand going to a lawyer, if she had to take it there. The money now belonged to her, and if where Chez now resided was any indication of where he would be for the long term, she knew that there would be no repercussions behind her decision.

She closed the safe and climbed back down the ladder. Neeta's next move would be to call the phone company and change her numbers to an unpublished one. She giggled as she happily padded through the house. Chez's last words to her suddenly came to mind. Remember, don't let me down, Neeta.

Contorting her beautiful, grinning face into a nasty glare, she coolly mumbled, "Consider yourself let down, nigga, cause this loss is gonna have to be charged to the game."

Dresser sat and waited, nervously biting his nails as he thought of just how low he had gone to finalize his deal. Although his insides ate at him, he knew it was no turning back. It suddenly hit him with the force of a ton of bricks, that he had sunk to an all-time low when he agreed to deceive Boo-Boo in the manner that he soon would.

He jumped at the sound of what he thought was an approaching vehicle, but he received a momentary reprieve once he realized that it was only a false alarm. Wishing that he was anywhere besides where he now sat, Dresser couldn't help reflecting back on his earlier meeting with Mann, Supreme, and a large contingent of their crew.

Upon arrival at the spot they had designated, he had quickly informed them of his plot to bring the Third Ward into their control, if he was allowed to continue running it as a legitimate member of their organization. Though he feared for his life, Dresser figured that he held the trump cards that would make it not only foolish, but outright stupid for them not to bargain with him.

He held his breath as a tense silence befell the room at the completion of his statement. Dresser noticed the cold stares and indecision written on the faces of the assembled men. However, he was aware that there was only one person in the room that needed to give his approval, and with unblinking eyes, Supreme was who he awaited an answer from.

After what seemed like an eternity, but was only a matter of moments, Supreme spoke with a piercing dangerous look in his eyes. The words that flowed so smoothly, yet carried a strong, demanding presence were words that Dresser would not soon forget. "Bring me Boo-Boo's head on a platter before the end of the night, and you have a place in our organization. Refuse to do so, and you will never leave here alive." Slowly inhaling a Cuban cigar, allowing the smoke to float from his slightly parted lips, Supreme calmly questioned, "Now, what's it gonna be?"

The crackling sound from the walkie-talkie that sat on the dash, drew Dresser's attention back to the present.

"Heads up, brah. You have company," was the message that followed behind the crackling sound.

Glancing through the rearview mirror, Dresser's heart began to beat violently out of his chest, as a nauseous feeling overtook him at the sight of Boo-Boo's arrival. Nervously counting the moments until the whole episode would be over and done with, he erratically mumbled, "They left me no choice, my friend. They left me no choice."

In his heart, Dresser knew that every man had their own choice to make, and his had been selfish and underhanded. Now the wheels he had set in motion were about to turn out of control, and it was too late to change the path that he had set.

As he turned into the dark back street, the first thing that caught Boo-Boo's attention was the absence of any streetlights. Although he wasn't too keen on meeting anyone in such conditions, Dresser was an exception to the rule; they were boys.

With the recent problems that had basically torn their crew apart, he had been laying low, awaiting an opportunity to retaliate. Upon receiving the call from his partner, Dresser, he had resurfaced to aid him in whatever way he possibly could.

Peering through the darkness around him as he cruised up behind Dresser's whip, Boo-Boo put the undercover hoopty that he drove in park. He glanced at the M-16 and twin Glock 9's that rested on the passenger seat. He reached out to grab them, then changed his mind due to it only being Dresser that he was meeting.

As he exited the car and walked towards Dresser's whip, an uneasy feeling that he just couldn't figure out, hit him. Ignoring it, he quickened his step, reaching the passenger door in a few swift movements. Surprised at the fearful, nervous look he saw in his man's eyes when he reached the door and found it to be locked, Boo-Boo held the handle and Dresser's stare until he saw his partner avert his eyes in a helpless, sorrowful manner.

Slowly backpedaling with a mixture of rage and disbelief darkening his features, Boo-Boo realized what was taking place. He attempted to run to his car and the weapons inside. He heard the tires squealing on Dresser's car as it quickly exited the street, as he came face to face with Mann and two others, who aimed assault rifles.

Coming to the sad conclusion that he couldn't make it, he surrendered to the inevitable as the street lit up with automatic weapons fire. His last thought was, *why did I have to go out at the hands of my own man?*

After brooding over Monya's deceit throughout the day, I finally limped through the dayroom and throng of inmates who noisily watched the news in a daze. If not for the fact that I needed to check in on Neeta's progress, the remainder of my night would have been spent the same as my day; in bed.

I picked up the phone and dialed Neeta's number. I couldn't help the sideways glance I tossed in the direction of the television as the noise level abruptly increased. At the same moment, I glimpsed Boo-Boo's picture and the roped off scene with the caption that read, "The city has reached its 112th murder of the year." My shoulders slumped when the operator dropped a double dose of bad news on me. "The number you have dialed has been changed to an unpublished number."

The heartbreak that I had experienced earlier was nothing in comparison to what I now felt as my body involuntarily froze up. My entire world and everyone within it had ceased to exist. First, Qwen and Sam were murdered, then, Dresser for some odd reason, seemed to have forsaken me. Monya and Neeta, not wanting to be left out of the mix, followed closely behind him. But Boo-Boo, my nigga, Boo-Boo... well he was my ace in the hole. He was the last of my true soldiers, which made one solitary tear slide down my cheek as I dropped the phone to my side.

I dragged myself away from the television and Boo-Boo's murder broadcast. I turned a blind eye and a deaf ear to everyone who consoled me on the loss of my partner as I made my way back through the dayroom. Along with his death and the numerous events that had transpired in my life lately, a part of me also died. The new Chez had been born in his place. I was aware that from this point on, shit would more than likely get much worse. The hatred I would carry through my days and nights would keep me strong. I would avenge myself and my people, and my enemies would suffer if it was the last thing I did...

Chapter 6

"Arrgh," Toshia groaned as she twirled around in the motel's mirror, scrutinizing her reflection. This had been her morning routine, and after trying on a number of outfits, she was still undecided as to what she wanted to wear. Although the form fitting Versace pantsuit and open-toed heels that displayed her perfectly pedicured toes made her look absolutely delicious, Toshia didn't know whether it was right for the occasion. She was already nervous enough after not seeing Chez for so long. The last thing she wanted to not make the best impression that she could when he laid eyes on her.

She still remembered how fine he was when she first met him and Qwen in the park. Toshia recalled how Qwen reached out to shake his hand and introduce her and her friend. "Toshia and Monique, this here is my man, Chez. Chez, meet Monique and Toshia." Qwen spoke.

Unfortunately, on that day, Monique immediately took charge, and reached out to grasp his hand. Then in the sweetest voice she could muster, she said, "I'm glad to finally meet you, Chez. I've heard of you forever," she stated, giving him a picture perfect smile. Toshia knew that whenever Monique went into that shy girl mood, she was claiming her prize. And with Chez responding in his smooth voice, "Where have you been hiding, and how is it possible that I haven't seen you before?" she could tell they was feeling each other."

Chez had showed at that time, that he was more interested in her friend, Monique, and forced her on Qwen. However, Toshia felt like fate had brought them back together for the relationship that should have been. Besides, Monique had shared every detail of Chez's sexual prowess in the sheets, and she was looking forward to verifying every nasty detail.

"Shit! I better hurry my ass up!" she wailed when her eyes sought out the clock and time.

She decided to wear the outfit that she had on. She really had no other choice. Chez's visit would start in 45 minutes, and it was a 30 minute drive from the motel to the prison, which meant she had to get a move on if she planned to spend the whole day with her man.

"Old girl must be on her way, huh?" Monty asked as he entered the cell and went straight to my locker.

I stopped shaving long enough to glance in Monty's direction. "Yeah, little mamas on her way, but why are you all up in my shit?" I questioned, pointing to my locker and the way that he was rummaging through it without a care in the world.

"Aw nigga, don't act like that! After all these years, you should be used to this by now," Monty laughed, showing a mouth filled with golds.

Inwardly grinning as I watched him return to his task with even more vigor than before, I shook my head and turned back to the mirror. My partner was crazy as hell. I began thinking back to the first time life had shined any light in this dark place for me.

I was making my way to the yard to get in some rec time, when out of nowhere, four niggas who I had beef with in the streets caught me on the pull up bars alone. I quickly braced myself to be jumped and stomped. Hell, they had the upper hand, and had it been reversed, either one of them would have won the ass whipping of a lifetime. But, just has we was about to lock heads, Monty and one of his homeboys stepped in.

"What kind of bitch ass niggas got to come in fours to handle one mutha fucker?" he asked jokingly. He looked at me and spoke. "You must be a Gorilla, that these pussies got to come at you like this."

Monty then turned around and stuck the largest of the four with a shank he had made out of a toothbrush. Me and his other partner joined the party, quickly putting in work on two more of the crew. Before we knew it, the COs were firing warning shoots for everyone to get down, and we were all hauled off to solitary.

From that day until now, me and Monty had been inseparable.

"You shouldn't even think of it as your locker, when you already know that what's yours is mine, and what's mine is mine!" he said, interrupting my thoughts.

We both erupted in laughter.

"No, really…" Monty began, as he found an opened bag of Chips Ahoy and took a seat on my table. "I had a taste for something that I didn't have, and I knew that you would have what I needed. Your rich ass always be having the best shit in your box," he added, chomping on the cookies like he was starving.

"Whatever!" I snapped, thinking that he was the rich one, and that I would be starving if it weren't for the dough that Toshia sent me whenever she could. "Just eat and shut up, while I get fly for my visit."

"Yeah?" Monty questioned incredulously as he stared at the cookie that he held. "Can you believe that this nigga would talk to me like that, and he ain't even scared to do so?"

"Okay, that's it… you got to go," I stated, fighting the smile that threatened to appear at any moment. "I got to get myself together, and right now you're distracting me, so take the cookies and roll out."

Balling his face up in mock anger as he stood, Monty said, "That's cool. You got that." As he made his way to the door, he added, "I've been thrown out of much better spots than this, and as long as I'm not leaving empty handed, I feel like I got the best out of the deal. Anyway, be sure to tell Toshia's little sexy ass that I said what's up." He gave me a sneaky look, winked his eye and closed the door behind him.

I knew that I would miss my dude when he left. There was never a dull day when he was around, and with the exception of Monty, I didn't deal with anyone else on the same level that I had dealt with Qwen, Sam and Boo-Boo. Just the thought of Monty's upcoming release and the remembrance of my dead partners saddened me. However, as I cleared my mind of them, the fact that I couldn't change what happened to them hit me like a ton of bricks. Not wanting to dwell on the past, I tried my best to think about the present as I finished shaving. Toshia would be here soon, and I didn't want anything to ruin our special time.

Whenever Toshia arrived at the enormous prison complex, it never ceased to amaze her that so many of her black brothers languished behind the walls and razor wire topped fences, while black women in the world were forced to accept what little companionship they could get from the few men that were left. The thought saddened her, and she wished that her brothers would get it together. Taking one last look in the mirror in order to check her flawless appearance, Toshia took a deep breath, blew it out and exited the rental car.

As she made her way to the prison's entrance, drawing stares from the many people that stood nearby, she hoped that a male officer was working at the front desk. Her pants were way too tight, and she knew that a female officer would only hate on her. This was one of the reasons why she went through so many pains to find the right outfit whenever she came to visit. Ever since she had begun to visit Chez at the prison, she had noticed that the female officers scrutinized the prettier females that came to see their men, much harder than the others. Being pretty and possessing a curvaceous body, Toshia dreaded this part of her journey to see her man the most.

Toshia released a pent up breath when she entered the prison and saw the young black male officer who sat behind the check in desk. She had dealt with him on a couple occasions, and knew that he wouldn't sweat her. With the exception of his light flirting and roaming eyes, which she smiled and dealt with, she found it easier to deal with him and the other males.

"Well good morning!" The officer stated with a bright smile as soon as Toshia walked up. "I haven't seen you in while," he added, reaching for her identification.

Although he had purposely rubbed her hand when he grabbed her I.D. card, Toshia still smiled graciously and replied, "I haven't been able to get here."

"I hear you. Shit, these niggas should be glad that they even get a visit." He laughed, and typed in her information.

The officer's words caught her by surprise, yet she fought to maintain her smile. She received her identification card back, and turned to walk off, but slowed her step when the officer's muffled voice reached her.

"I love the way you're wearing those Versaces, ma. That ass is so phat!"

Frowning, as she stared at him, she was about to give him a piece of her mind, then decided against it. She turned around and continued walking, accepting the disrespect and unprofessional actions from the officer. She was there to see her man, and she wasn't about to allow anything to interfere with what was most important to her.

I was amped as I entered the visiting room. All of the inmates wore the same dark blue jeans and light blue button down shirts, but I knew that I stood out from the rest by the way the many females eyed me with hungry looks. My wife beater tank top hugged my muscular chest like a second skin, and showcased the thick gold link chain and small diamond studded cross that hung from it. My waves flowed in thick circles around my meticulously edged up haircut, and I wore a pair of wood framed Cartier shades and crisp white Air Force 1's.

I felt like a million dollars, and my smile showed just how ecstatic I was, when I finally reached Toshia and enfolded her in my arms. I had missed her so much, and as we kissed as if our lives depended on it, I didn't want to let her go. I reluctantly released my hold on her, and we took our seats and feasted our eyes upon each other.

Unable to release her hand, I openly stared at her and whispered, "Damn, I missed you, baby."

"No more than I have missed your sexy ass," Toshia replied, chewing on her bottom lip. She seemed to devour me with her eyes.

As if we had had the same thoughts run through their minds at the same time, without warning, we both burst into laughter.

"What?" Toshia whined, smiling brightly. "What were you just thinking about?"

Allowing my eyes to roam over her appraisingly, I licked my lips and replied, "I was just thinking about how good you're looking, sitting up in here, and how much I want you! That's all."

"What's stopping you then?" Toshia asked, no longer smiling as she glared across the table at me.

I gave Toshia an under-eyed glance. I knew exactly what she meant, but I played dumb to her meaning. "What's stopping me from what, ma?" I asked, breaking our stare.

Toshia had no doubt that Chez had understood her unspoken invitation. This wasn't the first time that she had offered herself to him on a silver platter, yet unlike the many couples that she saw around them that did everything imaginable within clear view of the other visitors, for some reason he always denied her the pleasure that she sought.

"Baby, you know what I'm talking about," Toshia mumbled, nodding her head toward a far wall and small corridor that lead to an exit.

When I followed her eyes to the spot that she had indicated, I was at a loss for words. I saw an older homie with his girl pent up against the wall. She held onto the wall and wore a look of pure bliss as dude rammed himself into her from behind. She wore a long dress, and it was apparent that she had taken the time to cut a slit in it for the occasion. I too, would have liked nothing more than to bend my woman over and make love to her until she begged me to stop, but when I finally had the chance to sex her, it would be in a bed and not a prison visiting room.

When I turned back around, the look on my face must have answered her question loud and clear, because Toshia quickly stated, "Alright baby, you got that! I can wait."

"Thank you," I said grinning. "It won't be much longer, now. I promise."

"Have you heard something from your lawyer, Chez? What's going on with your appeal?" Excitedly leaning forward in her seat, she stared expectantly into my face as she awaited my response.

Sighing, I forced a smile, but avoided eye contact as I responded to her question in a way that allowed her to keep the faith that she thrived on, while allowing myself to maintain my dignity. Even though I had slowly began to lose my belief in the fact that I would ever be granted any type of reprieve, and would more than likely end up doing the remainder of my thirty year sentence, I refused to break her spirit.

"I spoke with him earlier this week, ma, and he said that there's been no response from the Court of Appeals yet." Seeing her smile waver, and the way that her shoulders slightly slumped, I said, "In this case, the way that Virginia's Appellate Court throws the majority of their cases out within the first ninety days, the fact that mine has been there for a couple years has to mean something, baby."

"Yeah, I guess you're right," Toshia said, exhaling. She reached for my hand, and gently began to massage it as she looked off into the distance. A moment of silence engulfed us before she said something that solidified my belief in her, and proved to me just how much she loved me and had my back. "No news is good news at times, baby. Although I really believe that you're going to win this appeal and come home to me, if we lose it, we're just going to have to shake it off and go back at them from another angle. Just know that I love your ass, and I haven't invested the last few years of my life into you, to give up if things don't go as planned. Whether you like it or not, I'm here for as long as it takes."

Though I very seldom found myself in the position that I was in at that moment, I was at a loss for words. The words that Toshia had spoken, along with the look of genuine sincerity that showed in her eyes, blew my mind. There was nothing that I could say that would express my love and the gratitude that I felt. Thus, as I leaned into her and gently held her face in my palms, I allowed my lips and tongue to speak for me.

We spent the remainder of our visit, simply enjoying each other. We laughed and talked about the things that were going on in our lives, and before we knew it, the time had come for us to separate. I always looked forward to walking into the visiting room and straight into the awaiting arms of my lady. Yet, there were no words to describe the feeling that comes over me when I am forced to watch her leave. Although we had a wonderful visit, and there was no doubt in my mind that she was with me one hundred percent, I hated to see my baby go. As we stared at each other across the room, so many words were silently spoken between us. Our looks said it all, and even though we were surrounded by other departing visitors, in our eyes no one else existed but the two of us.

Toshia blew me a kiss and mouthed the words "I love you," as she exited the visiting room. I watched her silhouette until she disappeared from view, thinking about how lucky I was to have her in my life. However, when the guard called for the next two men in line to come into the dress out room, I relinquished any further thoughts of Toshia and freedom, and followed the man in front of me into the room to be strip searched.

Though Toshia always hid her emotions from Chez as much as she possibly could, it took every ounce of strength that she possessed to hold back the tears that erupted every time she walked through the visiting room exit. The way that he had held her with such an intense stare while she waited to be escorted out of the visiting room ate at her heart. Toshia knew that he loved her, and she realized just how hard it had to be on Chez, to have to stand by and watch her walk away each time that she came to see him.

She wanted to take her boo home with her so badly. As she walked through the prison with unseeing, tear-streaked eyes, Toshia ignored the many people who openly stared at her. She was heartbroken, and in love with a man who she wanted to come home, but realized that there was a possibility that he never would.

She entered the rental, and attempted to get herself under control. As Toshia started the car and backed out of her parking space, her eyes stayed glued to the prison as she drove out of the parking lot. Though her tears still flowed freely, the words that flowed from her mouth spoke of the strength and resolve that lay within her.

"Just hold on baby! Everything is going to work out, and you're going to be released from this place. There's no way that God is going to bring us together only to keep us apart, Chez. We will just have to wait a little bit longer, baby."

Even as Toshia drove away from the prison, deep in the recesses of her mind, she allowed a glimmer of hope to exist, that one day she and Chez would make their journey together. No one could make her believe anything different, because in Toshia's mind, there was no other way.

Chapter 7

1997

I listened to Biggie Smalls', ready to die at a deafening volume while pumping the massive iron plates as if they weighed nothing.

It was all a dream,
I used to read Word Up magazine.
Salt'n'Pepa and Heavy D up in the limousine.
Hangin' pictures on my wall
Every Saturday Rap Attack, Mr. Magic, Marley Marl,
I let my tape rock 'til my tape popped.
Smokin' weed and bamboo, sippin' on private stock
Way back, when I had the red and black lumberjack
With the hat to match.

Although I was aware that I had more than likely passed my required twelve reps, Biggie's words had me in a zone that provided the extra push I needed in order to work my already bulging muscles to a state of exhaustion.

As I pushed the weight off my chest like a mad man, as usual, the past and all the turmoil I had experienced through the years found a way to come crashing back. With 30 years to do, and no real hope of coming from underneath it, weights had more or less become my method of escaping the reality that this life would be the only life I knew, for a long time to come. Nevertheless, like every other day I had woken up to in the last four years of incarceration, today would be no different. I would live it to the fullest, in the hopes that in time, my life as I once knew it, would be returned to me.

Feeling a tapping pressure on the bar, I glanced upwards, and saw my partner, Monty, grilling me. Grinning, I placed the weights back in the rack, raised up from the bench and removed one side of the headphones to hear what he was saying.

"Damn, nigga! Can someone else lift this shit with you or what?" he joked as he took up the position I had just relinquished with a smile in place, that boasted a mouthful of golds. Bracing the soles of his feet on the concrete, Monty grunted with the force of the heavy weight as he lifted it from the rack and began his set.

Spotting him, I watched the effortless manner he used as he went through each repetition. It suddenly occurred to me, that in the next few days, this would be a thing of the past. He was out of here, and after bidding side by side for the last three years, I knew that I would miss my partner terribly.

"Yo, Chez, get this shit," Monty hissed through clenched teeth and tensed, shimmering muscles.

I grabbing the weight, I erupted in laughter as I placed it back in the rack.

"You find that shit funny, huh?" he questioned mischievously, laughing at the situation, himself.

"Nah, brah," I explained, still chuckling. "Nah, it's not funny. I'm... I'm sorry, man," I apologized, catching my breath. "I got caught up in a thought for a moment. You know how it is sometimes, brah."

"Yeah, dog. You know I feel that," he replied, standing up and removing his weight belt. "Only thing is, whether I feel it or not, I'm not about to chance you getting caught in thought anymore today, while I've got over 300 pounds stuck on my chest." Playfully slapping my shoulder, he said, "Let's roll."

Tired and in need of a nice, hot, shower, I quickly agreed.

My mind was totally immersed in the letter I was writing, while thoughts of Toshia and how she had unselfishly been holding me down throughout my ordeal inspired me to flow on paper.

Out of all the women who had shared my bed, and capitalized in one way or another from my wealth, it never ceased to amaze me how the one woman I had never sexed nor gave a dime to, turned out to be an angel in disguise.

Regardless of how she happened to come into my life, Toshia was now my woman, and when it was all said and done, the last thing I ever wanted was to be without her. Turning my attention away from the letter and thoughts of Toshia at the sight of the flickering light, I saw Monty's profile in the doorway and removed my headphones.

"They just called us to chow. Come on, man," he casually stated.

"Alright. I'm coming," I replied, placing a pillow over the letter I had been working on, along with my radio and headset. Heading towards my secret hiding spot, I said, "Hold me down," as I retrieved my Plexiglas knife and placed it on my hip.

Never going too far without my knife, due to the ongoing beef we held with the Tidewater posse, I preferred the Plexiglas knife over steel ones, because of the ability to easily sneak them through the metal detectors that were positioned throughout the institution. On the first day that I came to the penitentiary, I decided that I wouldn't get caught slipping by any of the haters or hounds that roamed the yard in search of drama. Although I couldn't think for them, I clearly planned to butcher whichever one or ones, who were foolish enough to step my way. I would have no qualms about murdering anyone who thought it was sweet, because the only place I planned to die was in the street.

Our numbers had swelled to around thirteen heads by the time we reached the chow hall. It wasn't unusual for us to roll in such large cliques, since rolling tightly with our homies was instilled in everyone from the moment we touched down in the penitentiary. In some instances, day to day survival depended upon your strength in numbers.

Halting at the doorway, we each acknowledged the homies who were already seated in our large section. Scanning the sea of faces present, I quickly realized that even though the majority of our homies weren't there, we still presented an intimidating picture with at least 70 dudes already awaiting our arrival.

After collecting the bullshit that the institution gladly called a meal, we headed to the seats that had been reserved for us to sit in. "What's good, homies?" I uttered to two of my 3rd ward homies, who unknown to me, were in the process of interrogating a young homie from the block who had just arrived. Nodding in the direction of the newest arrival who I didn't know, I began to eat, as little portions of their conversation made its way to my ears.

"Who's getting all the dough on the 3rd ward these days, brah?" Poe anxiously questioned.

"Man, that nigga, Dresser, has that shit on lock," the new arrival retorted excitedly. "You wouldn't believe how hard he's flossing, homie. Since he hooked up with the nigga, Supreme, he acts like a fucking king around the way."

I immediately lost my appetite after hearing dude's statement. Jerking my head in his direction, I could tell that my partner, Little One, had caught the evil look that momentarily flashed across my face.

Silently signaling him with my eyes to chill, I placed my attention back on our young homie. "They're out there shining like that for real, brah?" I asked, breaking into the conversation.

"Hell yeah!" he squealed, raising his brow as if to say 'you ain't know?' "Them niggas have too much cake. Not only does Supreme be rolling in Bentleys and shit, even his girl be flossing in a Ferrari Spider. Pssst... I'd be full of shit if I said another motherfucker in the city was shining anywhere near as hard as dude."

I couldn't even front, I felt sick. The New Yorker had not only taken my bitch and money, now he controlled my block. Then, to hear how hard he was shining out there wasn't helping matters one bit. From the sounds of it, he wasn't lying when he had promised to take care of Monya. I couldn't believe that he actually had her riding around in a fucking Ferrari, whew!

Becoming angrier as I reflected on Dresser's snake ass, along with the bitch, Monya, I silently asked God to allow my appeal to go through. Snapping out of my thoughts, I barely spoke above a whisper with a voice that cracked with rage and resentment. "What does Supreme's girl look like, little homie?" After the question left my lips, I wished with all my heart I could take it back. I knew full well I really didn't want to know the answer, but it was too late.

Grinning foolishly, he shook his head with a dreamy look in his eyes, then closed them completely. "Oh shit!" he groaned loudly. "You have got to see her, man. Ole girl is absolutely fuckin' beautiful! Imagine the sexiest short, red bitch you have ever laid eyes on, then give her some long, black curls, and magnify shorty by ten. Yo, that's Supreme's girl."

My head was exploding at the thought of that dirty bitch, Monya, giving her all to the nigga I hated most in the world. She didn't even hang around long enough to hear the judge deliver my 30-year sentence, before sexing him like a dog in heat. For all I knew, she was probably fucking him before my shit had even started going sour. Having worked myself into a frenzy, I lost control, slinging my tray through the air with no regard for where or who it landed on.

Hearing the tray crash to the floor, Monty stared from where he sat a few tables over with a questioning look on his face.

I felt foolish. "My bad," I said to no one in particular. I cut my eyes in the direction of the new arrival, who stared from Little One to Poe with a dumbfounded look.

Strolling from the chow hall, even as angry as I was, the tinge of jealousy that tugged at my heart four years after realizing that another man was receiving all of the good loving that I had always prided as my own, was really hurting the shit out of me. At that moment, I would have rather died from the slugs Supreme had placed in my body, than the emotions that Monya's disloyalty had caused to brew inside me. Sliding back into a zone that I hadn't experienced in a long time, I hated the fact that I even cared. I had Toshia now, and in her, was a woman with a golden heart. But with every step I took, I wondered more and more what Monya was doing. Was life really as sweet for her as it sounded?

Holding her battered, swollen face, Monya laid in the fetal position surrounded by broken glass and overturned furniture. The loud, screeching sound of Supreme's Corvette careening down the long driveway drowned out her sobs, but presented her with a vivid picture of the many times she had found herself in the same predicament. Pondering for what seemed like the thousandth time, what happened to the Supreme who not only loved, but worshipped her, Monya wondered how she had gotten herself into this bullshit.

"Why me? What have I done to deserve this?" she whimpered in a voice that was barely above a whisper.

Though Monya was distressed, she had never shared her pain with anyone, figuring that her present suffering was nothing more than karma. After the way she had selfishly discarded Chez over 4 years ago, whatever agony she had suffered since, was more or less deserved.

It had never been this way with Chez. Even though he was no angel, with his constant whorish ways. He had never even acted like he would put his hands on her. Thus, with each beating that she tolerated at the hands of Supreme, it had become even clearer to her that no other man had ever loved her, besides Chez. Crying even harder at the realization, Monya concluded that her life would have been a lot better had she never left him. Chez would have kept her safe, instead of inflicting pain and anguish upon her. However, after what she had done to him, Monya knew that with him, was a place that she would never be again.

She had not only left him in his greatest time of need, she had played him for all the streets to witness. Maybe if everyone in Richmond didn't know that she was once Chez's and now Supreme's, she would have some hope, but Supreme had made it clear to everyone that he had everything that once belong to Chez!

"Get money, nigga," Monty loudly exclaimed, walking in the cell, waving a letter in my face. He tossed the envelope in my lap, shot me his usual gold-toothed smile, and made himself comfortable on the bunk.

"Fix that shit when you get up, nigga," I spat; cracking a grin and retrieving my letter.

Seeing the funds received stamp, along with Toshia's name on the envelope brought an even brighter grin to my features as I ripped open the seal. Quickly scanning the contents, I flipped to the ending and was elated to find that not only did she still love a nigga, she would be visiting in the next few days. I cut my eyes at Monty and decided to read it later, because of the way he was staring in my face with a mischievous grin. I realized that the jokes wouldn't be far behind, if I showed any sign of being pressed.

"Damn, Chez! What she say that got your soft ass all happy and shit?" Monty devilishly taunted, as soon than I placed the letter back inside the envelope.

"None of your business, nigga! You need to be worried about getting out of this joint in another two weeks, instead of what I got going on," I replied with a phony frown that quickly turned into a smile.

"Yo, don't do that, man," he stated with a serious look.

Immediately shedding my humorous demeanor, I asked, "What's up with that, brah? You alright?"

"I don't like to talk about leaving when you gotta stay," he responded, shaking his head disgustedly. "I hate that shit, man. A nigga be wanting to take you home too, brah," he confessed, raising his voice a few decibels.

"Don't start getting soft on me, little brah," I joked in an attempt to brighten the mood. "I need you at home, not here with me." Smiling to show more enthusiasm than I actually felt, I stated, "I've been home plenty of times. I was just too foolish to stay there."

With sincere eyes, he said, "You know I got you, right?" as he reached to give me a pound.

"Yeah, brah, you already know I do. Just don't count me out yet, though. I still have a few tricks left up my sleeve. Plus, a nigga needs to get back out there and handle some business." Slapping him a pound, I stated in a matter of fact tone, "I definitely have a few motherfuckers that I need to bump heads with, so in order to do that, I'm gonna have to get the hell out of here."

Monte smirked devilishly. "All you got to do is say the word, and me and the team will handle it. Hey, I owe you one, nigga! Anyone you have a problem with can easily disappear."

Momentarily pausing to reflect on his words, I decided that although it would be easy to have someone else handle my dirty work, this was something I needed to do myself. "Nah, partner, I'm good. However, if my appeal happens to come through, I'm gonna need you to have my back."

"That's not a problem, bruh. You get up out of here, and whenever you need me I'll be there for you. Believe that, Chez," he answered me.

I shook my head in response. No more words were needed. If I was ever able to return to the outside world, I knew that I could count on my newfound little brother and the team of murderers he commanded even from behind prison gates. Our bond was true, so now all I had to do was get out.

"Please! Ohhh! Ohhh! Supreme! Ohhh, stop. Supreme... please stop!" Neeta cried out loudly, in a hoarse, quivering voice. With tears clouding her eyes as her body forcefully crashed into his, she begged and pleaded with her insides raw and flaming. "Please take it out, Supreme! Oh my God...you're killing...me!" she yelled.

Oblivious to her pleas, Supreme continued to punish her as a slightly hysterical chuckle erupted from between his tightly clenched teeth. Wishing that it was Monya whose screams were booming in his ears instead of Neeta's, he continued to force himself into her tight ass over and over. Feeling his approaching climax, Supreme closed his eyes and slammed himself into Neeta hard and fast.

Holding on to the countertop as the searing pain felt as if she were being split in half, Neeta was too hoarse to scream. Whimpering her pleas between grunts, she had to swallow in order to force down the vomit that threatened to find its way to the surface. Unexpectedly, her torture came to an abrupt end when she felt Supreme shoot his load deep inside her, followed by a loud satisfied groan.

"Thank God," Neeta barely spoke above a whisper as she slumped against the counter.

"Now, that's what I call some good ass," he commented, pulling his dick out and slapping her roughly on her massive, right cheek. "You got that good, tight shit, girl," he taunted, wiping himself on one of her best towels and pulling his pants back up. He removed a huge wad of bills and threw some on the counter. Turning to walk away, he took one last look at Neeta's nakedness and teased, "I got a good mind to get me some seconds on that ass." He laughed at the fear that showed on her features as she raised up from her slumped position and began backing away with wide eyes and her palms held outward. He bitterly spat, "I got shit to do right now, but I'll take a rain check." Chuckling in a loud, threatening tone, Supreme headed out of the kitchen.

Frozen in place, Neeta nervously stood, with pain coursing through her rectum, and listened intently until she heard the door slam, signaling his exit. With tears streaming down her face, she shivered at the thought of what Supreme had just done to her.

Neeta's lip trembled as she thought about the person she had watched him become in the last few years. He was now the total opposite of the individual who had swept her off her feet in the beginning. What hurt the most, was that she couldn't even afford to leave him. There was nothing she could do, and he knew it.

Neeta was uncertain how she had fallen to the point where any nigga would even think to carry her in this manner. Just yesterday, it seemed as if she was on top of the world. Money for her flowed like water, only stupidity had quickly changed that, leaving her even worse off than before.

Though Neeta realized that turning back the hands of time wasn't possible, she knew that if it were, the shopping trips, vacations, and all out flossing she had done just because she could, would never have taken place. Crying even harder at the thought of her empty safe, Neeta felt sick.

It wasn't just the thought of what she had suffered at the hands of Supreme, or the fact that her safe was empty that made her feel sick on the stomach. Regardless of how much she tried to duck it, the thoughts of what she had done to Chez, and the disgust she knew he would have in her if he was able to see what she'd become, was more than she could stomach. Unable to control the vomit that erupted before she could reach the bathroom, Neeta clutched her stomach and plopped down upon the soiled carpet.

I placed the letter and envelope down on the desk, and reflected on how lucky I was to have Toshia in my life. Out of all the women I would have expected to come to my aid, she had been the least likely candidate. Yet, from the very first time I had met her in the park, with Monique and Qwen, I had recognized the attraction.

Nevertheless, she was here, and even though I truly loved her, I still didn't trust her enough to expose the secret of the 3 million dollars I still had safely buried. Monya and Neeta had taught me very valuable lessons. Therefore, if Toshia continued to remain by my side, it would be because she loved me for the broke Chez that she thought me to be, and nothing more. However, if I was able to rise up from my present predicament, her life would make a drastic change for the better, overnight. She deserved to be treated like a queen, and I would see to it that she was. Despite my love for her, I refused to be swayed from my position, at the moment. Enough beautiful women had already crossed me. Therefore, from the first visit when Toshia had unexpectedly popped back into my life, I'd remained leery of her motives.

At 5'3", and 138 pounds, her flawless brown curvaceous body was just what I had needed to fill my otherwise lonely existence. Yet, it was her years of patience, loyalty, and love towards me that won her a place in my heart. Thus, it was my heart along with my gut feeling, which swayed me to accept her as my woman.

Now I just had to remain patient. My appeal had just been sent to the Supreme Court, and my lawyer was arguing tooth and nail that, although I had been found unconscious in the car with two keys and a gun in the trunk, there was no way of proving that they were mine. All my vehicles had been registered in the names of other people, so my argument may not have been the best one, but it was the last chance I had. That being the case, all I could do at this point was wait. Maybe, just maybe, things would work out after all.

Chapter 8

Monty was not just my closest friend; he was my brother. Although I had been trying to ignore the fact that his prison sentence had been quickly ticking down, it was no longer possible to do so. The dreaded day had finally arrived, and because of it, I hadn't slept a wink the night before. Although I was happy for him, and wanted nothing but the best for him, a sadness like I hadn't experienced since the deaths of my partners overcame me when the reality hit me that within the next hour, he would be free, and nothing more than a memory in the institution.

My heart ached at the thought that I had to stay, while my dawg would soon be back upon the bricks. Though I prided myself on being a gangster, I was fighting with all that I possessed, to contain my emotions, and I wasn't quite sure that I could. Nevertheless, I stood and put my game face on when I heard my partner's name being called over the intercom. I knew that as soon as he heard the summons for his release, my room would be his first stop before he left. Thus, when I heard his loud voice calling out to different dudes as he strolled down the corridor, I braced myself for the inevitable.

"Man, wake your ass up and turn some lights on in here," Monty snapped excitedly as he walked through the cell door, carrying a heavy bag and dragging one behind him.

Turning towards him, I was shocked at the slight cracking sound that I heard in my voice when I said, "I'm up, and leave my lights alone."

"Yeah, whatever!" He dropped the bags and said, "These dudes are trippin' up in here, acting like I'm supposed to leave them something, when they know that all this shit is my dawg's!" Monty grinned, then pointed at me. "What you waiting on?"

I looked down at my Polo slippers and mesh shorts, even though I already knew what he was talking about. I glanced at the bags that lay at his feet, so that I wouldn't be forced to look at him. "What am I waiting on? Man, I don't know what you're talking about."

Before Monty could respond, the same officer that had called over the intercom the first time, could be heard again. The request for him to report to the Receiving and Departure department was given in a much firmer, more commanding manner.

"Yo, put some gear on, man. We got to go," Monty said, crossing his arms over his chest and holding me with an inquisitive stare.

Avoiding eye contact, I realized that I was being selfish, but I had made up my mind that I wasn't going to walk him to the door. It was hard enough for me to keep my composure as it was, and I knew that I wouldn't be able to watch my dawg walk through the door without losing my cool.

"Bruh, I can't walk you out," I announced, shrugging my shoulders. "I'm already too messed up as it is, man."

"Damn!" Monty exhaled, then said, "My bad bruh. I hadn't even thought about it like that, but I feel you though."

I didn't trust myself to speak, so I just shook my head up and down in response to his statement. At that moment, all I wanted him to do was turn around and leave. Like everything else that I went through while in prison, in time, I would be just fine.

Though I was unaware at the time, Monty saw the pain that I was trying to hide, and was dueling with his own. He hated to leave me as well, but there was no way to take me with him. Digging in his pocket, Monty removed a piece of paper and placed it on the desk. "These are all of my numbers, man. You can always get in contact with me through any of these, bruh. And if you need anything, and I do mean anything at all... don't hesitate to call me, a'ight?" he asked, giving me an unblinking stare.

"I won't hesitate, and I want you to take care of yourself out there. You hear me, man?" I stated, returning his stare.

"You know I will! Now give me a hug so I can get the hell out of here," Monty said, laughing.

The officer's voice boomed over the intercom once more as we shared a brief hug. Breaking our hug and banging fists, no more words were spoken between us as Monty turned and exited through the door. I watched him stroll down the stairs and exchange farewells with a number of homies on his way to the unit's exit. Before he walked through the door, he tossed one last glance over his shoulder in the direction of my cell. Though he couldn't see into the dark room, I wiped the tears that slowly ran down my face and watched my best friend disappear from my view.

If I had never understood the advice that an old head had given me years before, while I languished in the city jail, it was suddenly crystal clear to me. He had warned me to never forge any relationships with anyone that would affect me in a negative manner if they were to leave me behind. Although I had discounted him and thought him to be no more than a bumbling fool, his warning had come to fruition.

As I lay on my bunk and stared up at the ceiling, I made a silent vow to myself that I would never allow anyone else to get as close to me as Monty had. From that point on, I would place a protective shield up and concentrate on myself, and doing my time.

Chapter 9

It felt good to be free. After three years, seven months and twenty-three days in the joint, Monty found it hard to believe that he was really free, and surrounded by his childhood friends. He had only been in the city for two hours, and they were already deep in discussion about business, and how they were going to strong arm their way back into Richmond's lucrative heroin trade.

"Rob and some Dread nigga got the Northside on smash," E.J. stated nonchalantly as he peered down at his two-way pager. "They're doing their thing, but it ain't nothing that a few well placed slugs can't bring to an end."

Monty nodded his head in agreement, then turned to Lavar. "Will we have any problem with your cousin Lil' Turk and his team on the Westside? I've been hearing a lot about them lately, and family or not, we can't allow him a pass when we set this shit in motion."

"I'ma get at him and let him know what's up. If he can't see the greater good of what we're trying to accomplish, then I'll just have to get at him for real!" Lavar stated with a tone that left no doubt about his meaning.

"I feel you, brah. Let's allow that to be our last resort, because he is family, and for that reason alone, we have to use a level of finesse and diplomacy when we step to him. The others won't get that." Staring around him to make sure that everyone understood, Monty said, "Now, what's the deal with those fools on the Eastside?" Without even hearing Rolee's response, he knew from past experience that nothing short of bloodshed would allow them access into the

Eastside's heroin trade.

"Those young boys are a problem," Rolee stated, laughing. "They're not going to take any interference from us lightly, and their leader is trigger happy as hell."

"Who is he, and how can we get to him?" The wheels were already spinning in Monty's head as he awaited Rolee's response.

"Dude's name is Jason, and he keeps a team of young goons around him. They hold him down in the projects like he's the president, and everywhere they go in the city, they roll at least three cars deep." At the completion of Rolee's announcement, he hunched his shoulders as if he was clueless.

Pausing to think about what he had heard, Monty decided that Jason would pose the only real problem for him and his team. However, he was a firm believer that where there was a will, there was always a way to deal with any obstacle that presented itself. He just had to think on it a little longer, and he knew that it would come to him sooner or later. As far as Monty was concerned, every man had their weaknesses, so he would pay more attention to Jason than the others, in the hope that he would be there when the youngster finally slipped up.

Within the first week of Monty's return to the streets, he had begun the takeover that he had planned while in prison. Thus far, not one shot had been fired in order for him to reap the benefits of the numerous blocks on the Southside that were now back under his command. The dudes who had held them in his absence were easily persuaded to relinquish their control, and although they still continued to eat well, they had been forced to go on a diet.

With the Southside in order, Monty and Lavar cruised through Lil' Turk's West End neighborhood with E.J. and Rolee trailing close behind them. "So your little cuz has come up for real while I was gone, huh?" Monty asked as he noted the busy block and expensive vehicles that lined the strip.

"Yeah, the lil' nigga is bossing," Lavar stated shortly. Pulling beside a group of hustlers who were leaning against a white Range

Rover, he motioned for the tallest man out of the group.

Monty watched closely as the man approached their vehicle. It wasn't until he got closer that Monty recognized Lil' Turk. Standing nearly six foot five, there was nothing remotely little about Turk. The ice that glittered brightly from his long chain and the watch that glistened on his arm as it swung at his side, defined his height in the streets as well. Monty had to admit that Turk had done well for himself during his absence.

Reaching the car and leaning inside the opened window, Turk said, "What's up, cuz? Oh, shit! What's up brah?" he added when he noticed Monty in the passenger seat. "When they let you out, man?"

"I touched down about a week ago, playboy," Monty replied, giving Turk a pound.

"That's what's up though. You need something?" Turk asked, removing a huge roll of hundred dollar bills from his pocket.

"Nah, I'm strapped!" Monty announced. "But I do need to holler at you though. Get in and let's swing around the block."

Peering over his shoulder at his soldiers, Turk said, "You niggas hold tight. I'm a take a ride with my peoples." Making himself comfortable in the backseat of Lavar's DTS Cadillac, Turk asked, "What's on your mind, brah."

Not one for mincing words, Monty turned towards Turk with an iced grill in place, and said, "Your block is pumping harder than any other block on the Westside, and I want it!" Seeing the look of alarm that instantly registered on Turk's face, Monty stated, "You're family, and I'm going to make sure that you continue to eat like the boss that you are, but we got to have this block, and there's no limit to what I'm willing to do in order to get it." Monty gave him a moment to process the information, and then asked, "So what we gonna do, handle this like family or get off into some gangster shit?"

Turk couldn't believe what he was hearing. Never in a million years had he expected Lavar and Monty to come at him this way when he got in the car with them. He had looked up to the two men all of his life. That being the case, he understood that there was no way that he could successfully stand up to them if he chose to defend his block.

He slumped his shoulders and leaned further back into the soft leather seats. His voice came out in a whisper. "I'm in."

Monty had been home for two weeks, and thanks to his friends and his connect, the dough was rolling in so fast that he could barely count it. Although to some, it would seem like he was an overnight success, the last thing that Monty felt like was a winner. He had only accomplished half of the task that he had undertaken. With the Northside and the East End of the City still in the hands of others, Monty was extremely unhappy. After sending word to Rob and the Dread who he learned was Rob's connect from Kingston Jamaica, that he wanted to have a sit down, then receiving their refusal, it quickly became clear that they would have to resort to plan B.

Parked in the busy lot of the grocery store parking area beside the Caribbean restaurant that Rob's connect owned, Monty and Lavar patiently awaited their prey. They had been following the Cadillac Escalade that Rob and the Jamaican rode in for over a week, and Monty and Lavar had become accustomed to the many places that Rob and his man went. Their daily activities seldom changed from one day to the next, making them much easier to track than expected. Because of the position that they held, and the many vultures that moved through the city on any given day, Monty was somewhat surprised that they had been able to get so close to the two men without being detected.

Meanwhile, regardless of how hard he tried, they had been unable to catch their Eastside target slipping in any way. The young cat, Jason's ability to avoid all of the traps that he had set for him, baffled Monty. Just the thought of their refusal to meet, and the arrogance and flat out disrespect that Jason had shown their crew, caused Monty's anger to return ten-fold. Although he was aware that he would have reacted in the same way, Monty couldn't accept the way that Jason had not only refused his request, but threatened his life and the lives of his crew if they were to ever step foot into the East End again.

Monty didn't take the threat nor disrespect lightly. He planned to deal with Jason at the appropriate time, but at the moment, he was engrossed with the two men who he saw exiting the Jamaican restaurant. The two bejeweled men looked as if they didn't have a care in the world as they headed to their truck and got inside. The men had no idea that when the Escalade pulled out of the parking lot and merged into traffic, two cars pulled into traffic directly behind them.

Monty noticed a stoplight up ahead and said, "Fall back, Lavar. Let E.J. and Rolee get ahead of you." He stuck his arm out the window and waved his hand. Nothing more needed to be said. Everyone knew their positions, and the time had come to play their parts. Monty leaned further back in his seat and grinned at Lavar. He knew that in the next few minutes, the two men who were blocking his entrance into the Northside, would no longer exist.

Closing the distance between their Cutlass and the Caddy truck, E.J. turned to Rolee and said, "The next light is about to turn red. You ready?"

"Hell yeah!" Rolee's laughter boomed through the Cutlass as he leaned forward in the seat to get a better look at the stoplight. He was ready for action, and the Mini-14 that sat on his lap with the extended clip inside, carried more than enough firepower to handle the task.

Like E.J. had predicted, the stoplight turned red, and the truck's brake lights lit up as it slowly cruised to a stop. Making sure that he left enough room between the Escalade and the car behind them in order to navigate their escape, E.J. brought the Cutlass to an abrupt stop and reached for the SKS and the door handle at the same time.

They exited their vehicle, and running at a low crouch, he took the driver's side while Rolee ran towards the passenger's side. Moving with the speed and efficiency of trained assassins, they opened fire on their unsuspecting victims. Firing through the tinted back windows, their bullets ripped through the truck, raining shards of glass and metal. When the firing stopped, E.J. removed his clip and replaced it with another. He then opened the driver's door and emptied the remainder of the new clip into the already lifeless bodies. They prided themselves on being killers, and the last thing that they were going to do was allow any of their victims to miraculously recover.

"You should have been there. They were going back and forth as if they were about to exchange blows at any moment," Monty's lady friend of the evening talked nonstop, missing the annoyed look on his face.

Monty stared at her, wondering when she was going to shut up. She hadn't stopped to take a breath or give him time to respond to her, ever since they entered the restaurant. As he watched her intently, no longer listening to the words that escaped her pretty lips, it suddenly dawned on him that he needed to cut their date short. As much as he wanted to get her into bed and fuck her senseless, there was no way that he could put up with her constant chatter.

Sliding his chair back from the table and standing, Monty removed a large roll of cash from his pocket and peeled off a couple hundreds.

He tossed the bills on the table and sternly stated, "Let's go!"

"Excuse me!" the young beauty snapped, staring upwards with a questioning look. "I haven't even finished eating. I'm not going anywhere. You better stop trippin'," she added, rolling her eyes and mumbling under her breath as she began to pick at her uneaten meal.

Chuckling at the realization that she had no idea who she was dealing with, Monty shrugged his shoulders and walked off. He had only known her a couple days. After meeting her during one of his heavy spending sprees in the mall, she saw him flash his bankroll, and found a way to get closer to him. Therefore, he had no real ties to her. Her angry outburst behind him, failed to stop Monty or even slow his steps as he headed for the restaurant's exit. For him, women came a dime a dozen, and he had no doubt that he would have another to replace her before the day's end.

As he walked outside and hit the button on his keychain to deactivate the alarm on his car, Monty's attention was suddenly drawn to the swaying backsides of two women who had exited the restaurant in front of him. They were both blessed with the type of curves that he loved, but the much shorter, lighter complexioned female who held the hand of a little girl caused him to do a double take. Though her companion was beautiful in a ghetto sort of way, the one who held his attention was model material. Thinking that he had found the replacement for the date that he had just left behind, Monty was about to call out to her when he saw her point her key ring towards a white Maserati and start the ignition.

Immediately halting his step and spinning to look around him, Monty reached beneath his shirt and grasped the handle of his .45 Ruger as he observed his surroundings. The women's bodies no longer held any importance to him. The only thing that mattered to Monty at that moment was the car that they were getting into. As he quickened his steps in an attempt to make it to his own vehicle, Monty couldn't believe that he had stumbled across Jason's Maserati. However, as the car passed him and headed out of the parking lot, there was no mistaking who it belonged to. The rims and personalized plates gave the owner's identity away.

Monty followed the women as they hit the highway, and drove further away from the Richmond city limits. He trailed the Maserati for about twenty miles before they exited the highway. They led him on a wild goose chase through a series of winding roads before entering an exclusive Chesterfield suburb. It was clear by the look of the houses that they passed, that it took an abundance of cash to reside in the neighborhood. Monty slowed down when he saw the women pull into a circular driveway and exit the car. What he saw next, as he cruised past the house caused his adrenaline level to increase. The little girl ran into the outstretched arms of a man as he exited the three-car garage.

Monty had seen more than enough, and as he turned the corner and parked in an empty driveway that had a for sale sign on the lawn, he grabbed a fitted hat out of the backseat and pulled it down low on his head. With the last remnants of the sun fading from the sky, Monty hopped out of his car and jogged back around the corner. He didn't have time to take any precautions or call for backup. He had Jason right where he wanted him, and Monty was going to take advantage of the situation while it was favorable to him.

Monty breathed a sigh of relief when he crept into Jason's yard and saw him leaning over a motorcycle without the child, Monty stealthily moved into the garage. He was so quiet, that Jason didn't even know that he was there until Monty tapped him on the back with the butt of the gun. Although he realized that he should have just pulled the trigger and left as fast as he had come, he wanted to look Jason in the eyes and give him the chance to know who murdered him before he took his last breath.

"What the fuck is wrong with you?" Jason spat, then his eyes grew large.

"Yeah, you never expected that we would meet like this, huh?" Monty laughed, pushing the gun into Jason's forehead. "The last time we met, I was staring down the barrel of your gun. Now, look what you made me do."

Accepting his fate, the fear that Jason had shown upon seeing Monty suddenly turned to anger. "Nigga, fuck you!" With fire in his eyes, he growled, "Either kill me or get the fuck out!"

"Wrong answer," Monty spat.

He pulled the trigger, spraying brain matter all over the pretty candy painted motorcycle. Before the echo of the gunshot had faded, Monty was gone. With Jason's death, the last piece of the puzzle had been added, and with the Eastside now in his grasp. The city was his for the taking.

Chapter 10

1998

Experiencing a mixture of shock and exhilaration, I sat upon the bed with my head cradled in the palms of my hands. After five years of waiting, I was free. My lawyer had come through for me, and although I had dreamed of this day for as long as I could remember, I had honestly never expected to win my appeal. If anything, the thought of winning my appeal had only been a way of coping with the everyday hell of captivity.

Smiling, to halt the tears that threatened to come at any moment, it hit me that all the plans stored inside my mind were now able to be put into action. The same people, who had so easily deceived and hurt me years before, would now tremble at my return. Vengeance would be mine. Rising from my seated position, I scanned the cell that had been my home throughout the years. I grabbed a few mementos and walked out.

Though I already had plans to make life a lot easier for my homies on the inside when I touched down, seeing them coming to walk me out tugged at my heart. Nothing mattered more than reclaiming my life on the outside. However, after sharing my space with my homies for so long, it felt crazy to be leaving them behind.

Toshia was a bundle of nerves as she waited outside the prison. Unable to believe that Chez would soon be free, she continued to check her appearance in the visor mirror, between nervous glances at the prison gate. Though she honestly knew that she presented the perfect picture, this was the first time that they would be together without guards and visitors swarming all around them.

Pausing from her examination, Toshia bit her thick bottom lip in thought. Being realistic, she, like so many other women in America had done her share of trooping for niggas while they did their bids. Also, like her female counterparts, she'd had her heart broken by those same niggas who she'd basically bent over backwards for. Would Chez be the same? Had she again put her life on hold just to be kicked to the curb? She hoped that this time would be different.

She bowed her head and whispered a short prayer. "Dear God, please don't allow the love that I've found in my boo, Chez, to have only been a mirage. Let him love me just as much in freedom as he has while in captivity, because I've grown to need him like the air that I breathe." At a loss for words, her voice trailed off as she opened her eyes and slowly viewed Chez exiting the gates with a bright smile and eyes that seemed to be searching her out.

Visualizing one of her greatest dreams through tear-streaked eyes, Toshia hopped out of her car and ran towards the outstretched arms of the only man she ever truly loved.

"Shit!" Dresser hissed loudly, tossing the pool stick on the table, along with five crisp benjamins. Grabbing his drink from the edge of the pool table, he angrily stalked back to the table and the women who sat watching their game.

"I whipped that ass again, huh, nigga?" Supreme laughed, counting the twenty-five hundred dollars he had beat Dresser out of in an hour's time. "You want some more? I could always use a little extra money, as big as my trick bill is. What? You're not gonna let me get anymore of your loot, son?" he jokingly taunted.

"Whatever, nigga!" Dresser remarked, frowning. "I got my own damn trick bill."

Laughing even harder, Supreme had to agree. Dresser did trick just as hard as he did. Only, as good as Monica's pussy and head was, Supreme concluded that his boy was searching in all the wrong places. He basically lived with one of the biggest freaks in the city. Approaching the table, he decided that he would send Dresser to New York real soon, so that he could spend some quality time with Monica himself.

He dropped down into the empty seat between the two strippers they were supposed to have been interviewing for the club. Supreme tossed his winnings in the center of the table. "Here's the deal..." he began, eyeing each of the women in a lustful manner. "I want you bitches to get real freaky for this dough. If you agree, there will be no holds barred. So what's it gonna be?" he questioned with a raised brow.

"There's never any holes barred when we put it down," the slightly taller, lighter complexioned stripper chimed in as she reached for the stack of bills and thumbed through it. Finding the amount to be more than worthy, she cut her eyes at her partner, then stood and seductively began to sway her extremely well put together frame. She slid her form fitting dress over her head. She wore nothing underneath, but a lace thong that was wedged so far between her large ass cheeks, that it was out of sight. She smiled devilishly over her shoulder, and made each of her ass cheeks bounce simultaneously.

"Umph, girl!" Dresser loudly remarked at her short display of booty control.

Ignoring his abrupt outburst, she bent forward, grabbed her ankles and proceeded to make her large red ass clap violently. Continuing the shimmering, clapping motion, she reached behind her and unsnapped her tiny panties, allowing them to fall at her feet. Exposing her fat pussy and tight, brown asshole to the onlookers, she smirked. "Pick a hole, because unless one of you have a problem with it, I'm ready to get this party started."

Supreme liked what he saw bent over in front of him, but for some unknown reason, he found the dark exotic looks of the other stripper who quietly sat beside him even more enticing. Although she was a little more petite than her partner, she was still a dimepiece, and he sensed a tiger in her.

Licking his lips, Dresser stood and released his dick from his pants, interrupting Supreme's thoughts. "Yo, which one you want?"

he anxiously questioned, darting his eyes from the delicious red sight before him back to Supreme.

Supreme pulled his large dick out as well, and watched the exotic beauty beside him stare downwards with wide eyes and a slightly parted mouth, before unconsciously running the tip of her tongue between her teeth.

"I'll take this one," he said, gently reaching over to grab the back of her head and effortlessly guide it between his legs.

He noticed the ecstatic grin that sat on Dresser's face, as he wasted no time approaching the bent over stripper. He too grinned at the ravishing deep throat motion the female in his lap was attempting. Closing his eyes at the sensation she was giving him, Supreme, realized that he wouldn't trade the life he lived for any other. This was the way a nigga was supposed to live, and he planned to keep doing it just like this.

Deep in thought, I lay in the bed, puffing a blunt as sounds of music and the running shower pierced my senses. There were so many things that I needed to do, now that I was home. But, before any of them could be done, the first thing I planned to do was make love to my woman. Unfortunately, Toshia had decided to put on a Keith Sweat CD, and as Keith and Jackie screamed the lyrics to "Make it Last Forever," I couldn't help but to visualize Monya singing Jackie's part

Let me tell you how much I love you
Let me tell you that I really need you
Baby, baby, baby, I will make it all right
No one but you, baby
Can make me feel
The way you make me, make me, make me feel

Whoa...oh...oh...oh...oh...oh...
Mmm...mmm....mmm...
Don't let our love end (Don't)
Just make it last forever (Oh, make it last) and ever (Forever)

Monya used to love this song when we first got together. But I knew that was a long time ago, and we would never make that song real. So the only thing on my mind now, was extinguishing the fire that raged in Toshia's center. I had my own reasons for detouring from the prearranged plans, and having her stop on our way up 1-95 and rent a hotel room. I figured that she would be angry when I sent her home to Washington, DC alone, I decided to go ahead and send her there a little less upset, with a sore pussy, and the knowledge that her man had fucked the hell out of her.

Snapping out of my thoughts at the sound of the shower going off, I anxiously awaited the good loving that I'd never had, but had been dreaming about for so long. Somewhat nervous, I found myself wondering if I still possessed the necessary skills to please a woman. I was definitely out of practice and I knew it. But, as good as my boo was looking, I had little doubt that I wouldn't have too much of a problem finding my way through the maze. I placed the smoked blunt in the ashtray at the sound of the bathroom door opening. I prepared myself for the long awaited sight of my lady.

"Di...did you save...me some of that weed? I smell it..."her words trailed off at the unexpected sight of her man lying in bed naked, with his hands behind his head.

"Damn, baby!" she whispered, running her wide eyes over every inch of Chez's body. Sighing lightly, Toshia openly stared at his frame in awe. She was frozen in place at the vision of him lying before her with so many cuts, rips, and muscles covering his frame. But it was the large, thick muscle that rested against his thigh that really held her gaze.

Immediately beginning to moisten in anticipation, she slowly advanced into the room. Toshia had always wondered what made Monique so crazy about him. Now, she no longer had to wonder. As big as Chez's dick was, she could easily understand the attraction. Unfastening the towel, she let it fall to the floor, revealing herself to his hungry eyes. No longer nervous, she covered the short distance between them and melted into the protective arms that she had fantasized about for years. Feeling his lips devour her mouth, Toshia's last coherent thought was, 'Dreams do come true after all'.

Supreme hated to leave the two strippers with Dresser, but the important phone call from Mann was worth cutting his little freak show short. Walking towards the club's exit, he decided that by the way their bodies were locked together in a twisted embrace of licks and slurps, they wouldn't be going anywhere, anytime soon.

Having already left orders with the bouncers to not allow them to leave until he returned, Supreme grinned at the thought that they had no idea how hard they would have to work for his $2,500 dollars. Before they left the club, his whole crew would have the chance to freak them.

Arriving at the spot in record time, Supreme steered the Bentley down the warehouse ramp and stopped at the huge bay doors. He glared upwards into the security cameras that were mounted above the entrance, and immediately heard the remote device open the doors.

Mann looked towards the entrance at the sound of the bay doors opening. Surrounded by fifteen members of their crew, he stood grilling angrily as sweat poured from his chest and arms. Dressed in a wife beater, silk Versace pants and Versace slip-ons to match, a platinum chain with a large diamond cross dangled from his neck.

He turned his attention back to the unconscious, bloody, body that hung from the rafters. "Wake his ass up, Dax!" he spat.

Supreme parked beside Mann's 600 Benz, quickly exited the Bentley and walked over to where the action was taking place. "Look what we got here," Supreme stated, smiling as he unbuttoned and removed his Versace shirt. He decided that the last thing he needed to do was get blood all over it. He handed the shirt to Tee.

Coughing violently due to the bucket of water that had been thrown in his face, Butter awoke and stared at them through swollen slits. A mixture of fear and pain covered his features, as his body twisted in midair.

Grabbing a handful of Butter's braids to stop his swaying motion, Supreme roughly snatched his head back so that they held eye contact. "Damn, son, you don't look so good!" he angrily taunted. "I guess you thought you could hide from me forever, huh?"

"Nah, Supreme, I... I... swear, I was gonna call you," Butter stuttered. "Man, I didn't know that was your spot," he fearfully added in a whining tone.

"Yeah, I know you were gonna call, Butter." Supreme responded in a mocking tone. Then, without warning, he reared back and punched him in the mouth. "When, motherfucker? When were you planning on calling me?"

Spitting blood, Butter began to talk fast in an attempt to save his life. "Come on, Supreme. You know I would never knowingly cross you, man! Everyone knows you're the king around here, dog. Please let me make it up!" he pleaded. "Give me a little time, and I promise to make the debt right. Please!"

"Where the fuck is my eight bricks?" Supreme roared, tired of playing games. "There's nothing else your ass can tell me, nigga." Slowly pronouncing his words so that Butter would hear and understand every syllable, he asked again, "Where... is... my shit?"

Butter dropped his head and began to cry. He realized he was doomed. After balling out of control with the money from Supreme's product, other than a few grand, all he had to show for the robbery was clothes and jewels. Defeated, and aware that he was a dead man, Butter's sobs intensified.

"Yeah, that's what I figured," Supreme stated, shaking his head. He snatched the .357 semi-automatic from Tee's shoulder holster and said, "Since you took my shit, you can take these too." Squeezing the trigger, he watched as Butter's body jerked repeatedly with the force of the rounds from the powerful handgun.

Observing his work as the echo from his last shot rang out, Supreme neither blinked nor showed any emotion when he turned and handed Tee his weapon back. Without a second glance in the direction of the mutilated corpse that swung from the rafters, Supreme retrieved his shirt and put it on. "You niggas clean up all this blood, and do something with his body. When you're done, meet me up at the club." Walking back towards the Bentley, he informed them, "I've got two new freaks in the house that you niggas got to sample."

He grinned at the sour looks he saw reflected on the faces around him, jumped back in the Bentley and exited the warehouse.

Watching the Bentley as it exited through the huge bay doors, Mann was aware of just how much his cousin had changed in the last few years. It was at times like this that he really felt that Supreme was losing control. Like so many niggas before him, money and the power that it provided had turned him into someone else. Though they had all grown rich and powerful through Supreme's connections, Mann now wished that he had never sent for him to come to Virginia in the beginning.

Between all the coke and heroin they were overflowing the city with, and the many murders their crew had been responsible for over the years, it was only a matter of time before their show ended. Staring at all the blood, intestines, and brain tissue that sat on the warehouse floor, Mann could feel the end getting closer and closer.

Even though there had never been a doubt in my mind that I had lucked up on a winner when I got Toshia, after watching her sleep peacefully beside me, I decided that she was definitely a keeper. As my eyes roamed over her naked frame, it was impossible not to reflect on just how good her sex had been. Just as I had predicted years before in the park with Qwen and Monique, Toshia's sex game was nothing short of extraordinary. In no way had I been let down.

Glancing through the slit in the curtains, I noticed that the sun had gone down. We had spent the majority of the day in bed, and if I planned to get anything accomplished, I'd have to get up. Reluctant to do so, but realizing that I had waited entirely too long already, I gently removed her head from my chest and rolled out of bed. Picking up the articles of clothing I had hurriedly discarded earlier, I tried to dress as quietly as possible, but found my efforts to be useless when I heard Toshia's drowsy voice behind me.

"You going somewhere, Chez?" she questioned in a half sleep, panicky voice.

I looked over my shoulder and saw that not only was Toshia awake, she was lying on her side, staring questioningly at me. Turning back around so that I wouldn't see the look of disappointment I knew would be on her face, I said, "Yeah, baby. I have to go handle something real quick."

Toshia removed a leg from beneath the sheet and anxiously replied, "Okay. Give me a few minutes to freshen up, and I'll come with you."

"Nah, baby," I said stopping her in her tracks. "Stay here and get you some rest. By the time you wake up, I'll be back." Seeing her frown as she opened her mouth to respond, I quickly added, "I promise you it won't take long, ma."

Toshia exhaled and climbed back under the sheet, before timidly stating, "I guess this means we're not going home, right?"

Silencing her with my eyes, I ignored her question and finished dressing. I could understand that she was probably thinking a million different thoughts as her eyes followed me around the room. Realizing her position more than she knew, I attempted to ease her mind by walking to the bed and placing a soft kiss on her sweet lips.

I pulled away and looked deep into her eyes. "You know I love you, right?"

Tightening her lips to control her emotions, she whispered, "I love you too, boo. It's just..." she paused to wipe a lone tear. "I want to get you away from here. I've created a new life for us in DC, and all I want is for us to go home, baby." No longer able to catch the flow of tears that cascaded down her smooth, brown cheeks, she said, "There's nothing here for you anymore, Chez."

She wiped her tears while cradling her head against my chest. A part of me realized that every word she said was true. Only, whether she spoke the truth or not, I had a lot of past grudges that I needed to even the score on before I could even think about leaving Virginia. I knew to alot of people this seemed crazy, considering all that I had going for me at that moment. But I also knew me, and it was no way I could happily start my new life without fully closing out my old. Even if it cost me everything.

I released my hold on her, stood and grabbed her cell phone and car keys. "I got to go baby, but don't worry, alright? Believe me, I've got everything in order," I informed, using my index finger to gently brush a tear from her cheek, before heading towards the door.

"Please be careful, baby," she pleaded in a concerned voice.

"You know I will, girl. I got this," I grinned, and walked out the door on a mission to reclaim the most important thing of all. My dough. I only hoped that my money was still safe.

Chapter 11

Sticking the shovel into the hard packed dirt once more, I used my free hand to wipe the layer of sweat that had formed above my brow. I knew this had to be the spot, but after being away for so long, I was beginning to second guess my memory. Plus, the fading light and freezing weather was beginning to wear on my nerves.

I plunged the shovel into the ground again and again, I couldn't help but think about the possibility that I was ass out. Just maybe, someone else had discovered my fortune. Trying to remove such disastrous thoughts from my mind, I began to shovel even faster. I heard a loud 'clinking' sound with the next plunge. It was clear that the shovel had connected with something solid. Excited, yet nervous, I anxiously strained my eyes as I stared into the hole to see if what I had found was the treasure that my future had been built upon.

I dropped to my knees and used my bare hands to remove the caked on dirt. Beneath it, was one of the airtight canisters that held my millions.

Smiling harder than I had smiled in years, I feverishly began to remove the dirt. All my plans were about to come together. At this point, I realized that every dream I had once kept hidden in the recesses of my mind would soon become a reality. With 3 million dollars at my disposal, my enemies were now about to feel my wrath. The time for my revenge had finally arrived, and I planned to make it so sweet.

Smoking on some exotic green, Monty relaxed in the comfort of his newly acquired home. Surrounded by his crew, who along with himself were paid to the point where their days were basically filled with nothing more than drinking the finest liquor, smoking too much weed, and battling each other on the PlayStation for large stakes. Home for a year, so far, Monty had reclaimed his throne and all that came along with the position. With Lavar, E.J., and Rolee by his side, wiping out all opposition hadn't just been easy; it had been fun.

After the numerous turf wars and street trials they had experienced through the years, he had no doubt that they were the niggas who would hold him down through any situation, without question or regard for themselves. Virtually unopposed in the city, after reaffirming their position through murder and mayhem, they ruled over one of the most lucrative heroin operations in Richmond's history. Like their names, Southside's 16th street was known and respected by all who played the game in the city.

"Monty." the female voice loudly called out.

Snapping out of his thoughts at the sound of his name being called, he glanced at his newest plaything, Cherell, standing in front of him with a pair of tiny shorts on that left nothing to the imagination.

"What?" he snapped, as his eyes traveled from the fat mound that pressed at the tight material of her shorts, past her flat midriff, to a pair of 38C breast that threatened to burst from the confines of her shirt.

"Here, baby!" she exclaimed, blushing at the way he had lustfully eyed her private parts. She placed the phone in his hand, turned, and seductively swung her hips as she exited the room with every eye plastered on her undulating backside.

Shaking his head while watching the gestures of the other members of his crew, Monty concluded that she was most definitely a top competitor amongst the other dime-pieces he had. He decided to keep her around for a while. He raised the receiver to his ear. "Yeah, what up?" he spoke into the phone.

"What's up with you, motherfucker?" came the sharp, almost

threatening response.

Pulling the receiver away from his ear and frowning angrily, Monty prepared to hang it up, then thought twice, hoping that maybe the gangster on the other end would be tough enough to say his name. He would gladly go see whoever was violating his phone, if they were bold enough to put a name to the slick ass mouthpiece.

"Who you say this is again?" Monty questioned with a chill to his voice. Hearing laughter on the other end, his anger increased another level.

"Nah, brah, chill. It's only me, man. Yo, this Chez, nigga."

"What's up, nigga?" Monty quickly replied, with all traces of his previous anger absent from his voice. "Who you got on the other end, man, cause I know you weren't able to call this line collect?"

"There won't be any more collect calls for us from now on, playboy. I'm free as of this morning, little brah."

"Don't play, nigga! Say word," he said, dropping the joystick and immediately forgetting about the game he had been playing.

"Word, nigga. I'm serious, man. I got out this morning and this shit feels good too."

"Where you at, dog? I can't have you walking around out here looking like a 1993 reject. I'm gonna come scoop you up and take your raggedy ass shopping," he cracked.

"Nah, bruh, the last thing you have to worry about is your boy looking raggedy. I think I pretty much have the shopping money covered. I do need to get with you tonight, though. Give me a couple hours to handle something first, then I'll give you a call, alright?"

"That's what's up! But what you need a nigga to get you? Whatever it is, you know I got it," he said, excitedly.

"As a matter of fact, I do need something. Does that Iranian motherfucker you use to talk about still have those car dealerships?"

"Who, Zoo? Damn right he does!" Monty replied.

"Cool. Then give him a call for me and tell him that you're gonna be bringing your man through tonight. I need some wheels, and I plan on having them before the night is over."

"Oh yeah!" Monty laughed. "Well I hope you're not planning on riding too big, cause I'm not spending all my loot on your ass."

"Money is one problem I no longer have, slim. Make the call, and I'll get back with you a little later. I'm out."

Hearing Chez hang up, Monty smiled as he peered into the quizzical faces around him. Dropping the phone in his lap, he said, "That was my nigga, Chez, I've been telling you all about. He's home, and now that he's here, he'll be needing my help. Shit is about to get real wicked around here, which means that if I'm gonna have his back, I'm gonna need you niggas to have mine." Making eye contact with each of his childhood friends, he already knew the answer but asked anyway. "Are you niggas with me or what?"

The big, devious smiles that crept upon their faces at the completion of his statement, made any more words unnecessary. They would ride, because they loved the thrill of putting in work. Monty also loved it. Yet, unlike his crew, the closeness he shared with Chez made the shit more serious than usual. For him, it was personal this time around. Therefore, when his nigga said he was ready, the murder game Monty planned to unleash would be like no other their enemies had ever seen.

I returned to the hotel and found my boo asleep and looking just as delicious as she was when I had left her a few hours ago. "Toshia. Baby, wake up," I playfully urged, cutting the lights on.

She turned over, and slowly opened her eyes to acclimate them to the light. She smiled and said, "Hey, baby."

Locking my eyes on the smooth brown breasts with chocolate colored nipples showing above the covers, it dawned on me that I could get used to waking her on a daily basis.

"Baby, what you got in the bag?" she questioned, sitting up with an attentive look on her face.

Ripping my eyes away from the lovely sight before me at the sound of her question, it dawned on me that she'd had the ability to make me forget that I even held a bag, much less three million dollars. Glancing down at the bulky bag, I smiled. "I'm carrying our future, ma."

Staring from me to the bag with a quizzical look, she also began to smile.

Deciding that her curiosity level had to be at an all-time high, I figured that it would be cruel to keep her waiting any longer. I unzipping the bag and dumped the sea of bills on the bed as I watched Toshia's eyes grow wide as saucers.

"Oh... my... God!" were the only words that came out of her mouth as she watched the stacks of money pile up on the bed. Crawling from beneath the sheet that covered her nakedness, she gasped in a state of shock. Toshia cut her eyes in my direction and mumbled, "Ba... baby, where... did you get all this money?"

"It's mine," I said, laughing at the shock that showed on her face. "They thought they had broke me, but as you can see, I had something put aside for a rainy day."

"Damn, boo! How much money is this?" she asked, running her hand over the stacks.

Suddenly aroused at the sight of my boo's nakedness surrounded by all my money, I mumbled, "It's three million dollars," as I began to undress.

Realizing what I had in mind, she smiled, revealing the seductive 'come get this pussy' look that I found to be a true turn on. She swept her arms across the bed to clear a space, laid back, and spread her legs wide in an inviting manner. Speaking through slightly parted lips, she whispered, "Come and get this pussy, daddy."

A glimpse of the tight, pink center that sat deliciously before my eyes, made my already erect member jump in anticipation. Targeting the moist butterfly lips that hid her marble sized clitoris, I licked my lips as I hastily discarded my last article of clothing and dropped down at the foot of the bed. I crawled between her legs, clamped my lips over hers and began to lick and suck them, paying equal attention to the both of them while cupping her soft ass in the palms of my hands.

"Oh... my... God!" she groaned loudly, feeling her juices escape the confines of her pussy, only to have them mix with those already on my tongue. Gasping for breath with each flick of my talented tongue, she involuntarily rotated her hips, crying out my name each time my thick, wet tongue slipped inside her center.

I sucked her clitoris between my teeth as I parted her hairy lips with my thumb and index finger. I was astounded by just how good her juices tasted. Allowing her loud moans to be my indication of exactly what method I needed to use to make her cum, I placed more pressure on her clitoris.

"Oh shit! Chez, what... are... you doing... to... me!" Toshia groaned, trying to crawl away, but unable to do anything besides toss her head violently from side to side.

Locking her thighs in a vice like grip, I could tell by the way her body was bucking uncontrollably that her orgasm was coming. I placed a finger inside her pussy and began to manipulate the spongy spot of flesh that sat just above her opening.

"Shit!" she screamed, raising her voice to an ear-splitting shriek. "I'm cum... cumming! Damn... my pussy is... cumming, baby!"

I felt her body shudder uncontrollably as she pulled at my ears in an attempt to pry my mouth from her private parts, I listened to her half hysterical cries, knowing that phase one of my fuck game had been a success. The second half was about to jump off now.

I rose from between her legs and pulled her still spasming body to the end of the bed. Not even giving her a chance to catch her breath, I placed her thick brown legs over my shoulders and pushed them together as I entered her. In this position, her already tight pussy became a glove. Although I had never used this position before, by the way her eyes were rolling back in their sockets as she threw her head back and howled my name over and over, I knew it was working. I had to clench my teeth and concentrate with each stroke, because whether the shit felt good to me or not, this wasn't about my satisfaction.

Before I finished with her and allowed her to leave, she would know that the pussy and the woman connected to it, belonged to me. Beginning to sweat profusely, it dawned on me that I may be a little late for my rendezvous with Monty, but this was important. After five years of patiently waiting to handle my business, I figured a couple more hours couldn't hurt as I pounded into my lady with a vengeance.

Monya sat on the couch, in the spot that she had begun to feel rooted to. Lately, the couch, television, and their home seemed to be the extent of her existence. Disgusted with her plight, she pointed the remote in the direction of the huge television and began to surf through the channels. Bored and irritated, the remote surfing only served to make her angrier than she already was.

She raised her arm to fling the remote at the 60-inch screen, but she slung it to the floor instead, knowing that a good ass whipping lied ahead if she were to do what she had really wanted to do. Getting up, Monya mused that these days it really didn't matter what she did; Supreme's crazy ass whipped her whenever he felt the urge, anyway. It was a normal occurrence, so Monya more or less figured, what the hell?

She strolled to the terrace doors that looked out over the grounds of their estate, and peered down at the scenery she had once loved. What had once personified her dream home, now only resembled a prison. Scanning their property, Monya spotted numerous guards walking Rottweilers with weapons slung over their shoulders. She couldn't help but to wonder who exactly they were trying to keep away from the property. Although Supreme was never home anymore, as far as she was concerned, he was the one who they should have been keeping away. Actually, Monya was more than aware that she was the one they were there to keep an eye on. Escape for her, wasn't even an option.

Suddenly feeling depressed, Monya slumped back down on the couch. Balling up in a fetal position, she began to reflect upon the thought that had plagued her mind continuously as of late. Why did she leave Chez for Supreme? It was at times like this that she kicked herself for making such a foolish decision. Sighing as she relived the mistake through misty eyes, she knew that things could have turned out so differently. The question was, now that it had been done, how could she possibly make it right?

Wondering where Chez was and if he was alright, Monya decided to locate him and try to make amends. She truly doubted that he would understand, but she realized that even after all these years, he was the only man she had ever loved. After all the time that had elapsed, she couldn't help but to wonder how he felt about her. Unable to restrain the tears that cascaded down her face, Monya already knew exactly how Chez felt. He hated her, and although she missed and loved him, the last thing she could do was blame him for harboring such hostile feelings towards her. As she had grown to understand, some things were just beyond her control.

Chapter 12

Toshia walked into the apartment and exhaled as she dropped down on the couch. It had been a long trip. Though she wasn't necessarily tired; making the two hour drive with 2.5 million dollars in the trunk kept her on edge the whole way. With the constant police presence on 1-95, having so much money in such a close proximity had been scary. Then, to make matters worse, Chez had sent her home alone when she thought they would be making the trip together.

She realized that there were things he needed to take care of, but she couldn't quite understand why he had to begin them today. He was rich. Glancing at the bag that sat in the floor, she came to the conclusion that whatever he had to handle couldn't have had anything whatsoever to do with money. Deciding that it wasn't her place to second guess him, she figured that whatever was going on, would be dealt with however he saw fit. With that thought fresh in her mind, Toshia pulled herself up from the couch and moved to follow the instructions that had been given to her before leaving.

As she dragged the heavy bag through the apartment, she couldn't help but to grin at the thought that as long as she held his riches, there was no doubt that her baby would return. Still tingling from the Olympic sex he had blessed her with earlier, her grin broadened. The pleasure she had experienced bordered at unbelievable proportions. Slowing her pace to allow her aching arms a slight break, she couldn't help wondering where he was and what he was doing at that very moment.

It felt like old times again as I chilled with my dog. The feel of butter soft leather beneath me brought back memories of a past life that I can honestly say I never thought I would experience again. The old school Isley Brothers CD that flowed so smoothly through the state of the art system, had me on cloud nine.

Driftin' on a memory,
Ain't no place I'd rather be,
Than with you, yeah.
Lovin' you, well, well, well

Day will make a way for night
All we'll need is candlelights
And a song, yeah
Soft and long, well

Glad to be, here alone
With a lover unlike no other
Sad to see, a new horizon
Slowly comin' into view, yeah

I wanna be living for the love of you

Smiling, with a mouth full of glittering gold teeth, Monty teased, "Raise your ass up, brah, this ain't no damn cab!"

Too high to do anything but smile in response, I retrieved the blunt from his outstretched hand, turned the music up a notch, and continued to bask in my newfound freedom. It helped to know that by now, Toshia was at home following my instructions to the letter. Therefore, if everything went exactly as I wanted, when I finished my task, we would ride off into the sunset like a player was meant to do. I was rich, and I planned to be even richer before it was all said and done. Motherfuckers owed me, and what I was owed had to be paid. Although they weren't aware, their time had arrived to be held accountable for their deceitful actions.

Though I hadn't given Toshia any specifics, she knew that a new life was right around the corner. Unlike the majority of hustlers who dreamed of getting money and moving to Atlanta, I was thinking on a major level. Once my reign of terror was completed, Montego Bay, Jamaica, would be our destination, and it wouldn't just be a vacation. I planned to be there in no more than 30 days, and for the remainder of my days I'd be living the life of a true baller.

Pulling into the car dealership, Monty turned down the music and said, "What you see, brah? I know Zoo, has something you want on this bitch."

The Arab had a top of the line dealership, and as I looked around, I felt like a little kid in a candy store. "Damn!" I blurted, eyeing every make and model of luxury car imaginable as we parked. I was used to some big toys in my time, so it wasn't surprising that the 600 Benzes and 740 Beemers jumped out at me first. However, as much as I was tempted to purchase one of the showstoppers, the shine and attention they would bring wasn't quite what I was after at the moment.

I turned to stare at Monty, and gave him a serious look, before stating, "I see all the shit that's been in my dreams for years, player."

"I'm sure you do," he chuckled. "But you better have some dream money if you plan to roll off the lot with one of these beauties."

Laughing along with him, the only thought that traveled through my mind was *if only you knew how much money I really have*.

Dresser sat in his regular section of the club, surrounded by the usual crowd of sack-chasers and flunkies. Raising his champagne glass, he quickly drained the liquid in one fluid motion before tilting it towards one of the strippers who stood nearby to refill it. Giving her a look of indifference, he began to sip from the glass as he peered into the crowd. Dresser no longer received joy from being treated like a Don by all the fools that catered to his every whim. This stemmed from the fact that he already knew he was the shit. How could he not be the man, when his money said different?

Scanning the club as well as the activity taking place around him, he had to admit that Supreme employed the baddest bitches the stripper industry had to offer. With the exception of a small few, he had fucked them all. With that being the case, they were forgotten no sooner than the thought came to mind. However, the one his eyes settled on at that moment, grabbed his attention in a major way. Banging his iced out medallion against the table as he leaned forward to get a better glimpse of her goodies, he thought that she was exactly what he needed.

He licked his lips, while allowing his mind to wonder whether the many stories he had heard about her were true. Dresser concluded that he had waited long enough to get at Neeta. First, Chez had held her down, then Supreme had come along to pick up where he left off. Now that Supreme had moved on to bigger and better things, Dresser was prepared to shoot his shot. He had no doubt that he would be hitting her before long, he just needed to figure out exactly what angle he would use to get up in her. After draining his glass, he sat it on the table and stood. The time had come to work his magic.

Neeta took a seat at the bar and ordered a double shot of Hennessey. Good liquor was the only thing that helped her perform the degrading duties attached to her job. It was bad enough that she had to parade around half-naked, but being groped by low budget hustlers that wouldn't have even thought about stepping to her once upon a time, kept her drinking. Stripping to her was nothing more than a job that happened to pay well, but as Neeta turned up her drink, she found herself shaking her head at what her life had become. Who could have thought that shit would get this bad for her? She definitely couldn't perceive such a life for herself five years ago.

To add insult to injury, just when she thought Supreme was gone over her, he put her ass to work in the club and began to openly flaunt fresh, young bitches in her face on a regular basis. Having to witness his antics daily burned her up on the inside, mainly because at one point, he had treated her like a queen. It had been her good pussy that he could never get enough of. Now, regardless of how hard she tried, she couldn't get him to pay the slightest bit of attention to her.

Getting a shot of dick from the nigga was totally out of the question.

"Neeta, Neeta, Neeta," Dresser chanted in a smooth, sing-song voice. "What's up, baby?"

Snapping her head in the direction of the voice, with a nasty scowl plastered upon her features, Neeta was ready to insult whatever unwelcome intruder she encountered. Seeing Dresser standing behind her changed her mind. Even though conversation hadn't been on her agenda, she reverted straight into diva mode as she appraised his gear.

"Oh, hey, Dresser," she said with a slight trace of seduction in her tone.

Appraising her as well, Dresser extracted a huge knot of bills, more as a means of letting it be known that money wasn't a thing, than in preparation for buying her a drink. "What you drinking, baby girl?" he questioned, noticing the way her eyes lit up at the sight of his bankroll.

Openly eyeing Dresser's money, Neeta shifted her body on the stool so that he had a clearer view of her cleavage and glistening thighs. "It's Cristal for me, love," she said with a subtle lick of her glossy upper lip.

Smiling inwardly, he thought, Yeah right, but turned to the bartender and said, "Bring me a bottle of Cris." After the way she had stared at his money, and went on to do a mental calculation of his jewels, Dresser decided that getting in her pants would be a lot easier than he had previously thought. Grinning, he had to remember that she wasn't the same Neeta from the past, because if she was, they wouldn't be in a strip club holding a conversation in the first place.

She reached for the bottle, and he allowed a trace of a smile to appear at the corner of his mouth at the reality of the situation. Regardless of what once was, they were here now. Whether she had changed or not, she was on the verge of getting fucked.

Summing up the monetary worth she saw Dresser so blatantly advertising, Neeta decided that he was doing damn good for himself. From the looks of it, she concluded that the stories she had heard about him getting his weight up once Chez had taken the fall were true. The iced out medallion that damn near hung in his lap, along with the Rolex that looked like it had just been removed from a glacier proved that his money was long.

She reached for the glass of Cristal that Dresser had just poured for her, locked eyes with him, and gave a lingering smile. As she raised the glass to her moist lips and began to sip, it was clear by the way his lust-filled eyes traveled over her body that her night had just taken a turn for the better.

Zoo turned out to be just as cool as Monty had said he was. I liked dude on sight. Like myself, he was about his paper. After laying my eyes on the burgundy Navigator with peanut butter leather interior, it was a wrap. The truck was fly, but the light tint that covered all the windows was a plus. If nothing else, what I needed more than anything was to be on the low. I wasn't quite ready to let my enemies know that I had emerged once again.

Prepared to finalize the deal, I reached in each of my socks and emerged with two ten gee stacks. I tossed them on top of Zoo's desk, reached in my pockets and retrieved twenty grand more. I smiled inwardly at the look of astonishment that was pasted on Monty's face.

Glancing from the money that sat on the desk and back to me, Monty teased, "Damn, brah, you must have hit the lottery today!"

"Yeah, I guess you could say that," I winked conspiratorially, then reached in another pocket and removed ten thousand more. Tossing it on the desk beside the other stacks, I turned my attention to Zoo and casually stated, "That should cover the asking price, and I would appreciate it if you would throw in a set of 23 inch Polo rims, my friend."

Gathering the stacks and tossing them in a drawer, Zoo grinned. "You want Polo rims, then Polo rims it is," he informed, standing to shake my hand. "I'll have it ready for you by tomorrow evening, Chez. Monty, I need to have a word with you before you go," he said in a manner that spoke volumes.

I excused myself from what I felt was none of my business, and headed out the door. Returning to the car, I took the time to check out my little brah's whip. The silver GS, sitting on a set of 20 inch Lexus chrome rims was hot to death. Televisions were situated in every head rest, but the screen that sat in the dash was too nasty. I had to admit, my fam was doing real well for himself. I was proud of him. He was as real as they came, and he had shown me love by keeping his word and holding me down when he returned to the world. Now it was my turn to extend the same helping hand. What I had in mind was more major than he could imagine. When I saw him coming, I entered the car and made myself comfortable.

Monty hit the automatic start button as he sat in the driver's seat and whipped out into traffic. Searching for his B.G. CD, he shot me a devilish grin. "You're gonna be riding real big tomorrow, brah, but you can't do the factory thing when you're in a Navigator. What you gonna do about your system?"

"I hadn't really thought about it, man. Being that you're going to pick it up, just take it and have the joint fitted with the state of the art shit. Get everything you think I need and I'll hit you back with whatever it costs."

"You just may regret giving me the green light, cause I'm about to drop some major dough tomorrow, baller." Smiling, he joked, "Your ass needs to shoot by the mall and get some gear, because any nigga who can afford to sling fifty grand for a truck, damn sure doesn't need to be wearing Reebok Classics and penitentiary sweats."

Scanning my gear, it dawned on me that he was right. A change of clothes was warranted, but at the moment, it wasn't at the top of my to do list. I had more important issues to tackle, so shopping would have to take a backseat. "I'll get to that real soon, but do you have another whip I can use?"

"A cell phone and a burner will help a lot too, if you have them, until I can cop my own."

"Not a problem, my man. Not a problem at all," he said, pointing at the glove compartment as he began to hit different dials on the dashboard.

Finding a phone inside, I wondered what the hell he was doing. Then, as if on que, the whole dash slowly began to slide forward. I raised my brow as the contents came into view. I couldn't believe the arsenal he was riding around with.

I leaned forward to get a better view, and peered at enough weapons to begin a small war. There were two .45 Rugers, an AK 47, an SK and the biggest chrome automatic I had ever laid eyes on. Curious, I removed the mystery weapon and scrutinized the scope in amazement.

Giving him a confused look, I asked, "What the hell is this, dog?"

"A bad bitch is what it is!" he commented with seriousness in his tone. "That's my baby, brah. It's a .357 automatic with an infrared scope. Wherever the beam shows up on a motherfucker, they are about to be missing a body part. Believe that!"

"Oh yeah!" I grinned devilishly. "This bitch is mine now, brah, and I love her already," I stated, laying claim to my new girlfriend. "Now, what's up with you giving me a whip until my shit gets right, my nigga?"

Shaking his head, Monty said, "I got you. Damn! You haven't even been home 24 hours and you're getting on my nerves already!"

I laughed at his fake show of anger. It felt good to be back with my dog. Now it was time to bring the noise.

With Supreme out of town, Dresser had the run of the club in his absence. Relaxing in Supreme's office with Neeta, they polished off the last of their second bottle of Cristal.

He poured another portion of the cool liquid over his erect penis and stared down at Neeta's naked form as he squirmed from the expert treatment that was taking place between his spread legs. Instructing her through the process, he closed his eyes and enjoyed the feel of her warm, moist tongue as it lapped the champagne from his dick. His toes curled, and he had no choice but to agree that Neeta's head game was official. She was well into proving that at least one of the stories he'd heard about her sexual exploits was true.

Though Neeta was feeling the effects of the Hennessey and champagne, she was still well aware that if she played her cards right, Dresser's little dick ass could be the gold mine she was in need of. The thought alone made her increase her technique. Moaning excitedly, as if he had the tastiest dick she had ever sucked, Neeta took his whole length completely into her mouth and vulgarly began talking while her head bounced up and down.

"Ummm, Dresser! Damn! You're sooooo... big!" she lied, watching the way his eyes rolled back in their sockets. She ran her own fingers in and out of her center in a rapid motion, and whimpered, "You got me... so... wet!" With a suddenness that she had planned perfectly, she halted her actions and stood.

"What's wrong?" Dresser exclaimed, glancing at her with questioning eyes filled with lust. On the verge of cumming, he couldn't quite figure out what was happening.

Ignoring his question, she allowed her actions to give her response as she turned her back, grabbed the desk, and bent over in front of him. She spread her legs and raised up on her toes just right. Neeta stared seductively over her shoulder and purred, "Put that big thing up in me. Do it now, nigga!"

Eager to be up in her, no more words were necessary as he quickly moved into position. He parted her hairy lips with the tips of his fingers and easily sank into her sopping wet depths. He quickly received pleasure from her tightness, as well as her gasps for breath after each of his strokes. He began to move his hips in a fast pistoning motion. Hearing her loud moans, he cockily asked, "Who's pussy is this, girl? Huh? Tell... me... whose... pussy... this is!"

"Ahhh... it's yours... Dresser!" Neeta replied, moaning and crying out as if the dick was killing her, but really not even feeling it.

If he hadn't been so busy grunting and breathing hard himself, he would have seen the look of boredom etched on her face. However, bored or not, Neeta planned to do whatever was necessary to get in his deep pockets. Thus, if it took her legendary head tricks to make it happen, or the dick milking muscles she was working his tool with at that very moment to get it done, the task would be accomplished. It was all about a come up with her; love, lust, and affection was a thing of the past as far as she was concerned.

After making some inquiries, I was able to find Monya's father, Doc's whereabouts. Me and him had always been real cool. I saw him emerge from a pool hall, and after a brief wait, I rode up beside him and lowered the window. "What's up, old man? You need a ride?" I questioned, smiling a devilish grin.

Peering through the open window with a menacing scowl, his features quickly registered a look of shock. "Chez, is that really you, son?" he blurted out in a confused tone, stopping in his tracks.

"In the flesh," I laughed. "It's cold out there, player. Come on, let's take a ride."

He got in the car and he shook his head in disbelief. "Damn, Brah, I thought you were through, man. It's good to see you, son!" Raising his brow, Doc asked, "Have you seen Monya or my granddaughter yet?"

Unconsciously wiping the smile from my face, I replied, "Nah, man. No one knows I'm on the scene yet, and right now that's exactly the way I want to keep it."

Shaking his head, a sudden look of sadness settled over his features. Exhaling, he looked me in the eyes and began to speak in a low tone. "Since you've been away, a whole lot has changed, as I'm sure you already know. I understand that my daughter didn't do right by you, but before she was your woman, she was my baby. You're my man, and the last thing I want to do is make excuses for her actions. It's impossible for me to imagine how you have suffered due to the decisions she's made." After taking a brief moment of silence to allow his words to sink in, he continued, "I'm asking you as a player not to hurt her, Chez. You're still my family and my granddaughter needs her mother, so on the strength of that, let my baby live."

The pleading look in his eyes won me over. That, and the fact that no matter how much I hated Monya, a part of me would always love her. "Yeah, alright, you got that, man," I said, understanding where he was coming from. "The only thing is, I'm gonna need you to do me a few favors as well," I informed, gauging his reaction.

"Anything, Chez. I'm in your debt, son-in law. Now, you want to tell me what it is you need from me, because if I'm the only one who knows you're home, it must be serious."

"First of all, I need to see my babygirl, Doc. I've missed her so much," I said, recalling the sadness her absence had brought me through the years. Growing angry at the thought, I added through clinched teeth, "I need everything you can tell me about the nigga Supreme, and his operation. His time has arrived, player. I got a date with that nigga, Doc!"

Narrowing his eyes into angry slits, Doc spat, "You will see Chanae within the next 24 hours, and it will be my pleasure to give you Supreme's information right now!"

Chapter 13

The blue Crown Victoria was quiet enough to hear a pin drop on the carpet as we sat behind the dark tinted windows in silence. Monty sat at my side, while Lavar and E.J. rode in the back. Rolee and three other members of Monty's crew sat in an exact model of the car we rode in, behind us. Everyone wore audio monitors with mouthpieces that sported earplugs. The plan had been to maintain radio silence until we were ready to set our mission in motion.

Thanks to Doc, I now knew where Supreme's distribution base was set up. From the intelligence that he had given me, it was clear that the heroin and cocaine was moved from the back room of the strip club. All the money from purchases and his numbers operation were also brought here to be calculated each day before they opened the club for regular business. Deciding that this would be the best place to strike my first blow, we staked it out for the first week so that everything would come off without any losses on our end. Now that the best plan had been decided upon, it was time to set it off.

Seeing that the coast was clear, I turned to Monty and covered my mouthpiece. "It's a go, brah. Give the order, and let's do this shit!"

Giving me a sinister smile, he spoke firmly into his mouthpiece. "Alright, fellows. Let's make this shit look official. Once we have them gathered up and cuffed, we can have a little fun." He popped his door, he chuckled, "Don't forget, we are federal agents, so follow Chez's lead."

Exiting the car with SK's in hand, we ran towards the club's doors with our ATF jackets swinging and the sounds of our booted feet echoing off the pavement. We reached the doors in a matter of moments. The largest member of Monty's crew slammed the heavy battering ram into them with a mighty force and brought them down. Between the thunderous sounds of the collapsing doors, tables overturning, and the yells of "ATF! ATF! Get the fuck down!" the scene was one of total chaos.

Not one shot had been fired, but my finger was glued to the trigger in the hopes that someone wanted to be a hero. However, from the looks of it, we had caught them totally by surprise. Bricks and money lay everywhere, and the constant clicking of the overworked money machines resounded throughout the room.

I cut my eyes at Monty, who stood smiling at my side. I saw his men cuffing niggas through unseeing eyes, but I heard his words loud and clear.

"We caught 'em slippin', brah! Now, let's make these ho's pay!"

I felt the exact way that he did, but the demonic look I witnessed in his eyes at that moment made me glad that we were on the same team. Nevertheless, regardless of who was on my team, I had set my vengeance in motion. From this point on, there would be no turning back.

Stunned, Monya bit her bottom lip in disbelief as her fingers moved over the keyboard in a blur. What she had stumbled across when she typed Chez's name and identification number into the Penitentiary Locator site was beyond her comprehension. Receiving the same response, she blinked in shock at the computer screen. Chez had actually been released. How it happened, she would never know.

Staring at the screen, it suddenly dawned on her that Chanae had done nothing but talk about her father all week long. At first, chalking up her ramblings as being nothing more than those of a six-year-old child, Monya knew better. At this point, she needed to know more, and only one person could supply the information.

"Chanae!" she yelled in an insistent tone. "Chanae, come here, baby!"

Running into the room with a doll in her hand, Chanae giggled excitedly as her attention shifted from her mother, back to her doll.

Gazing at her daughter, Monya couldn't help but to take notice of just how much she resembled Chez. She was a beautiful little girl, and Monya truly adored her. Patting her lap, she said with a heart-melting smile, "Come here, little lady."

Running as usual, Chanae hopped into her mother's lap and hugged her as tightly as her tiny arms would allow.

Monya hugged her back, then released her hold on Chanae and got straight to the point. "Mommy needs you to tell me something, and I need the truth, okay?" she asked in a soft, loving tone.

Nodding her head up and down, Chanae gave her mommy a big, bright-eyed stare.

"Alright. Now, you have to cross your heart and hope to die before we begin, because you know how serious this is, right?"

"Umm hmm. I know, Mommy!" she said, crossing her heart with a serious look etched across her features.

Taking a deep breath, Monya stared deep into her daughter's eyes. "Have you seen your daddy, sweetheart?"

Nodding her head 'yes', a big smile quickly surfaced upon her face.

"Where did you see him?" Monya asked as her heart beat out of her chest.

As if Chanae had been waiting for the chance to share her secret with someone, she opened the floodgates and innocently rambled on. "We went to the zoo and saw the animals, Mommy. Daddy took me to McDonalds, and we went to Skate Land." Smiling brightly, she breathlessly blurted out, "My daddy loves me, Mommy!"

Chez was really back, and Monya knew it. She had no idea what he had in store, but whatever it was, she knew it wouldn't be nice. Drifting off into deep thought, she decided that she needed to see him. Now, her only problem would be figuring out how to make contact. She knew that if he wasn't trying to be found, it wouldn't be possible.

Biting her tongue in thought, she whispered, "Chez, where are you?"

Supreme's men were cuffed and laid out on the floor in a line. There wasn't a nervous or fearful face in the bunch. Instead of being worried about the circumstances they now found themselves in, laughter and defiant taunts resonated throughout the room.

"You bitches can't hold us!" were the words that spewed forth from the angry mouth of the captive closest to where I stood, watching Monty's men toss brick after brick of product into large sacks.

"You hear me, motherfucker? Our lawyers will have us out before the end of the night! Then I'm gonna see you!" he growled, making a threatening comment for the benefit of his companions as I glared angrily in his direction.

Cutting my eyes across the room at Monty, I saw that all the money had been packed and we were ahead of schedule. This was good, because I needed a little extra time. Thanks to the loud mouth that was still shouting threats, I had suddenly come up with a new course of action.

"We're through!" Monty hollered across the room, adding, "Let's wrap this shit up, brah!" Quickly covering the distance between the loud mouth and myself, my smile slowly began to grow brighter.

Narrowing his eyes at my approach, he bared his teeth angrily, but was caught completely off guard when I swung my boot into his grill. The painful howl that escaped his mouth followed by teeth and blood, had quieted all the other taunts and laughter.

Removing my ATF jacket, I saw the once defiant eyes around me switch to wide, fearful looks as my crew pulled their jackets off as well.

With blood pouring from his parted lips, the loud mouth questioned in a panic, "Man, what the hell is going on?" He looked around with darting eyes. His once gangster demeanor seemed to have diminished.

I responded with a chilling look and laughed at the ex-tough guy, as I reached towards my back and retrieved the .357 automatic and fired two slugs at pointblank range into the nigga who laid cuffed up beside him.

Yelling as the blood and brains from his man's head splattered all over his face, he began to babble incoherently. "Oh, my God! Ooooh, shit!" he cried, trying to break free of his cuffs, along with the remainder of his handcuffed companions.

"Now, does that answer your question, bitch ass nigga?" Laughing in a loud, mocking tone, I nodded to Monty, and all hell broke loose as he opened fire on the helpless men. Their screams rang out loud and animal-like, yet they only lasted a matter of seconds once Lavar and the others joined in the massacre. The scene was savage, but the point I'd come to make was clear.

Other than the whimpering cries of the loud mouth, the screams and weapons fire were silent. I reached in my pocket and retrieved my switchblade. Looking down at the cowering figure, I spoke low and calm. "Today is your lucky day, player. I'm gonna let you live to tell your boss what happened here." Seeing the hopeful look on his face, I continued, "The only thing is, in order for me to let you live, I gotta cut your fucking tongue out for all that shit you were talking!"

"Huh?" he blurted loudly, looking around him for an escape route that didn't exist. "Come on, man! Please don't do this to me! I'm sorry--"

"Take it or leave it!" I flatly stated, cutting him off as I flipped the knife open and awaited his reply.

Tears slowly began to roll down his face, picking up speed as his cries increased. Slowly, his tongue began to creep past his swollen, bloody lips, indicating his submission.

Leaning forward with knife in hand, I heard a chorus of chuckles from Monty and his crew. With a straight face, I reached out to grab his tongue. It was at that moment that the realization actually hit me; Revenge is sweet when served properly!

Supreme watched over Mann and Tee as they weighed the 200 keys their Mexican connect had sent them.

"Everything's in order," Mann said, as Tee placed the two Fendi suitcases on the cart and wheeled them over to the table where Supreme sat with the two beautiful couriers that Fernando had sent.

"You'll find a million dollars in each of those," Supreme said, turning to face Consuela, who raised her drink in a mock salute. "Take a look inside."

Though she knew it wasn't necessary, Consuela quickly scanned through the contents of each suitcase, then polished the rest of her drink off and stood. Giving Supreme an appraising look, she winked and tossed a number on the table. "The next time you're in Miami, make sure to put my number to use." She cast him a flirtatious glance, and to guarantee that he would give her a call, she put an extra twist in her hips as she sashayed out of the room.

Reading the digits with little to no interest, Supreme balled the piece of paper up and tossed it into the ashtray. He was used to gorgeous women throwing themselves at him, so Consuela's number meant nothing to him.

Immediately placing his mind back on the kilos stacked around him, he grabbed his cell phone and dialed Dresser's number. Consuela and any other bitch would have to wait. Money was the only thing he had on his mind at the moment, and he knew that Dresser would want at least 50 kilos.

Receiving a beep on his other line, Supreme clicked over and snapped into the receiver, "What?" He listened to the urgent ramblings of one of his workers on the other end and immediately flew into a rage. "What the fuck do you mean they killed everyone but Chuck?" Cutting the person's reply short, he screamed, "Fuck him and his motherfucking tongue! If he allowed some niggas to just walk up in my establishment and rape me for half a million dollars, eleven keys of heroin and twenty-eight bricks of cocaine, he should have made them kill him along with the rest of them! Better yet, you kill him! And I want some answers about how this happened, immediately!"

Supreme ended the call and slammed the phone against the wall. He spoke to Mann and Tee in a cracking voice that resounded with fury. "I don't know what the hell is going on, but whoever did this is gonna pay! They don't know who they're fucking with! But when I find out who they are, they'll wish that they never set sights on our shit!"

God Forgives, The Streets Don't 2

Watching as Neeta slept, Dresser couldn't believe that he hadn't been home since the night they shared at the club. He was well aware of her track record, but regardless of how hard he tried, he just couldn't seem to get enough of her. The sex was everything that he had heard it was, and then some. Sliding from beneath the sheets in an attempt not to wake her, he reached for his pants.

"Where you running off to?" Neeta asked, yawning.

"I need to take care of a few things, but I'll be back as soon as I finish. Alright?"

"Okay," she mumbled, and leaned over to give him a kiss.

Breaking the kiss, Dresser immediately felt an erection as he stared into her hazel, lust-filled eyes. The fact that somehow the covers had lowered, leaving her beautiful naked body uncovered and open to his view didn't help matters any. He swallowed the saliva that created a pool in his mouth as he allowed his eyes to travel freely over every inch of her body. He wondered why she had pulled that shit when she knew he had business to attend to. She was well aware of the effect her body had on him, and he knew it.

Releasing a fake yawn, Neeta stretched provocatively, uncovering more of her nakedness in the process. Inwardly smiling at the way he gawked with his mouth open, she asked, "What's wrong, baby?"

He forced his eyes away from the delicious view before him and checked the time on his Rolex. He realized that there was no time for a quickie, but he wanted Neeta, and that was all there was to it. Dropping his pants back on the floor, he crawled back in the bed and continued their kiss.

As she hungrily returned the kiss. It was funny to Neeta that he was so weak. It was entirely too easy to play him. In the week since they had hooked up at the club, not only had he not been home, the nigga had been paying off like a slot machine.

Faking a moan as his hands traveled roughly over her body, she had to suppress a giggle at the thought of having sex with his baby dick. The way that she cried out and clawed at his back during intercourse had to have him feeling like Lexington Steele in the flesh. Amazed at her own acting skills, she knew that the way she put it down was worthy of an Academy Award.

She spread her legs to give him entrance to paradise, and prepared herself for another starring role. If she had it her way, this would be the mega payday she had been waiting for, so she wasn't about to let him get away.

"Nigga, your ass is too cold!" Monty roared in laughter, referring to the tongue that sat on the glass table in front of us.

Joining in the laughter with the others, I said, "The nigga was popping too much shit for me not to take it. Now, I believe he'll shut the hell up!"

"Yeah, I imagine he will!" Monty snickered, placing the money and dope we had taken into our respective bags. Lowering his voice a decibel or so, he spoke in a low tone. "I split everything up between the two of us. You have over a quarter million in the bag. The fourteen keys of coke and five and a half birds of dope will be shipped wherever you need my people to carry them."

I stared at my partner appreciatively, and smiled at the thought that even though he was on my team, he had no understanding of what I was really after. Drugs and the game no longer meant anything to me, and I had more than enough money to be comfortable for life.

"What the hell are you smiling about, all up in my face and shit?" Monty asked in a cheerful tone.

"You, nigga! I'm smiling about you!" I said, pushing the bag filled with drugs back to him. "You keep that shit and split it up amongst your people. I'm good, brah." Seeing the questioning look in his eyes, I boasted, "I'm rich, little brah! So that's exactly how I want to see you."

With a mischievous grin in place, he said, "If you insist. I think I can find something to do with this shit." Pausing, he added seriously, "We sent your man a vicious message today, Chez. It's not gonna be easy to catch them slippin' next time, so what's our next move?"

Having thought the same thing, I really hadn't come up with another course of action, just yet. As long as niggas were leaking in Supreme's crew, I was good. "I don't expect to catch 'em slippin',

I just want to catch 'em. So, check it. Keep niggas on the stakeout at their spots, and if we can catch any of the main players, we'll just pick their asses off one at a time."

"Alright. I'll keep my people on it. But if I'm calling the shots, everything I catch with New York plates is the enemy. Your beef is mine, brah," he informed with a fire in his cold, hard eyes.

Giving him a pound, there was no doubt in my mind that he meant every word he said. The nigga was loyal, and that's exactly why I loved him.

Ever since Monya had stumbled across the information that Chez was home, she had been a nervous wreck. The only thing that worried her was what was on his mind after brewing on her deceit for the last five years. She already knew that there would be some bloodshed, now that he was free. She only hoped that none of the blood would be hers. Sure, she realized that when he fell, she had rolled out with more than $1.5 million of his money. However, the plan she now had in mind would undoubtedly make up for her error.

With the combination she had to a much larger safe, secure in her mind, Monya decided that if Chez was with it, she would gladly give him the $5 million that Supreme held inside of it. Sighing at the task ahead, she wondered how she would get in contact with him. Though she concluded that he would show his face soon, she just hoped his face wouldn't be the last sight she would ever have the privilege of seeing.

Chapter 14

Rolee passed one of the many lit blunts around the MPV as they sat in conversation. Tired of just sitting around, the mood inside was tense due to their boredom. In charge of the day shift, Rolee's job was to oversee a team of four from 9 to 5 as they watched everyone who left or entered Supreme's other strip club. Rolee lived for action, which made sitting around for the last week in a van annoying, to say the least.

He turned around to retrieve the blunt that was being offered to him, and did a double take when he glimpsed the New York tags on the 600 Benz pulling up in front of the club. No longer interested in the blunt, it dangled from his fingers as he stared at the opening driver's door. Watching as the jewel-clad driver exited the whip, he couldn't help but notice the air of importance the driver carried himself with as he swaggered towards the club's entrance like he ruled the world.

Receiving a sudden jolt of excitement at the prospect of dude being someone important within Supreme's organization, Rolee tossed the blunt in the ashtray and grabbed his phone. He hurriedly dialed Monty's number. The only thought traveling through his mind was putting in work. Counting the rings, he watched the Benz like a hawk, and anxiously awaited the sound of Monty's voice, thinking that the last thing he wanted was for dude to escape his wrath.

Monty relaxed in the comfort of his newly purchased 5 Series Benz Coupe as he and E.J. cruised through the streets of Richmond. Life was great, and although money had never really been a problem, after the hit they had put down the week before, he now held the title of one of the richest niggas in the city. With eleven keys of heroin, and twenty-eight kilos of coke at his disposal, not many ballers in Richmond could touch him.

"Yo, brah. Those bitches we met in After Six last night keep blowing my shit up," E.J. stated, checking his two-way pager. "You want to slide through their spot and see what's up or what?"

Pausing to form a mental picture of the two Middle-Eastern beauties from the night before, a devilish grin came over Monty's face as he shot E.J. a mischievous look. "Yeah, that sounds like a winner to me," he remarked, already planning an evening of freaking. They were both certified dime-pieces, so the prospect of fucking them was interesting.

He smiled at the thought of adding to his already vast network of freaks. Monty felt his phone vibrating on his hip. He reached for it at the same moment that E.J. began to speak into his own. "Talk to me," Monty flatly said into the receiver.

"Brah, a dude just pulled up in a big 600 with New York plates, and I've got a feeling that he's somebody special in the nigga Supreme's organization. I gotta have him!" Rolee exclaimed excitedly.

Needing some drama in his life as well, Monty chimed in, "You really feel like ol' boy is sure enough affiliated with the dude, Supreme?"

"Hell yeah! Let me get him dog. Shit! The worst thing that could possibly happen is that we make the mistake of killing a New York nigga that's down here getting money and fucking bitches that belong to us anyway!" Rolee angrily spat.

"I guess you have a point," Monty laughed. "But let's have a little fun with this one though. Snatch him up and bring him to the empty house over in Blackwell. I'm gonna go grab Dozier and a couple of his family members and meet you there."

"Yeah, you do that," Rolee stated in a fit of laughter. "I'll take care of dude on this end. But damn, man! Dozier? You're a cold nigga, dog. The coldest nigga I know!" he added and ended the call.

Monty turned to E.J. and whispered, "Is that them?" receiving a nod along with a questioning look, Monty said, "There's been a change of plans, player. We'll have to take a rain check. We're about to have a little fun."

Shifting his attention away from E.J., a slight chuckle escaped his lips as he imagined what Dozier and the others would do to the New Yorker. He would have to grab his video camera when he picked them up, because this would be some shit that he couldn't resist getting on film. Excited at the thought of surprising Chez more than anything else, he couldn't wait until Rolee handled his end of the job so that the games could begin. After the way that Supreme had destroyed his man's life, there was no level that he wasn't prepared to go to in order to help return the favor. Payback was a must!

They followed closely behind the 600, Rolee made sure that his man kept at least three car-lengths between them the entire way. The last thing he wanted dude to do was get spooked. He needed the element of surprise to remain on his side in order for their plan to work.

Riding shotgun with an AR-15 on his lap, it had already become clear to him that if all else failed, he would take the New Yorker back to Monty within an inch of his life. His instructions had been to bring dude back. How he got there had been more or less left up to him.

Jerking his head in the direction of the Benz as it turned into a convenience store parking lot, Rolee's adrenaline began to flow. This was the chance he had waited for. Pointing at one of his men in the back of the MPV, he instructed, "You. Come with me." He cut his eyes at the other two men, and added, "Hold us down if needed, but if we don't encounter any problems, just follow us back to the South Side."

Nodding their heads simultaneously, everyone prepared themselves for the encounter that would undoubtedly unfold at any moment.

Oblivious to the MPV that pulled into the parking lot behind him, Unique parked, took one last hit from his cigarette, and reached for the door handle. The loud music that blared through his speakers made it impossible for him to hear the MPV speed up as soon as he stepped from the Benz.

Spinning around at the sound of doors opening, Unique frantically reached for his weapons at the sight of men running towards him. Their murderous glares left no doubt in his mind of their intentions. However, not even his lightening speed was a match for their determination, because as soon as his hand reached the butt of his automatic, something crashed into his temple. Immediately losing his grip on the automatic, all he saw was blackness before he fell to the pavement.

Working quickly, they dumped their victim's unconscious body into the back of the Benz and sped off.

Rolee felt a sense of exhilaration at the outcome of their stakeout, as he whipped out into traffic and away from the scene. Everything thus far had gone perfectly. Glancing through the rearview mirror into the backseat where his man sat with his gun to the head of the unconscious New Yorker lying on the floor, he cracked a smile. He retrieved the phone from his pocket, punched in Monty's number and placed it to his ear. Their next stop would be Blackwell, and Rolee couldn't wait to see Dozier do his thing.

Rolling through the South Side with my system knocking at a thunderous level, I felt like my old self. I was free, paid, and unstoppable. However, at the moment, I was also horny as hell due to the porn flick that was now showing on one of the many television screens that Monty had installed in my truck. As much as I hated to do it, I was tempted to snatch up a little freak and punish her. Only, on some real shit, I wasn't trying to carry it that way. After the realness my boo had shown me, how could I be anything besides real with her as well?

Just the thought of Toshia made me realize that after two weeks at home, I'd only seen her once, and that was the first day I came home. It was time to remedy that, and that's exactly what I planned to do as I reached for my phone.

As soon as I grabbed it, I was surprised to find it vibrating. "Yo!" I said into the receiver, somewhat irritated that my call to Toshia had been set back.

"Where you at, and how long will it take you to get to 16th?" Monty asked.

"I'm already on the South Side. Why? What's going on?"

"I can't tell you over the phone, but it's a surprise you don't want to miss," he informed me with a chuckle.

"Yeah, alright," I said dryly, wondering what the surprise could possibly be. "Give me ten minutes, and I'll be through. But Monty, this shit had better be good, 'cause I was on my way out of town."

"Be good?" he repeated. "Nigga, what I got for you is something great! And I promise you that it won't take long at all. Just hurry up!" he excitedly stated and ended the call.

I placed my phone back in the console and I whipped through traffic with Monty's words fresh in my mind. He had a surprise for me that I didn't want to miss. I had no idea what his surprise could be, but knowing him, it would be just that; surprising. Nevertheless, whatever it was, once it was unveiled, I was out. I had important business that needed handling, and before the day was over, I planned to take care of it. My lady and I would definitely be spending some quality time together, and nothing was going to stop that.

Taking the steep steps two at a time, Monty descended into the cold, dark basement with E.J. on his heels. Though their booted feet made little noise as they made contact with the old, creaking steps, the sounds of the three pitbulls that tramped beside them echoed through the stairwell.

"I see you niggas finally made it!" Rolee teased, meeting them at the bottom of the stairs. "I couldn't wait, so we had a little fun with the nigga before you got here."

Eyeing him suspiciously, Monty asked, "How much fun? You better not have spoiled the surprise I've got planned."

"Yeah, yeah, I know, brah. We didn't work him over too bad." Reaching for one of the dog chains, Rolee said, "What we did was nothing compared to what he's got coming."

Hearing footsteps, they looked up the stairs and saw Lavar and Chez heading their way. They greeted each other with hugs and pounds, and the five of them made their way further into the dark basement where more of Monty's men waited.

"Okay. Where's the surprise?" I questioned, staring around me at nothing but darkness.

My question was quickly answered when Rolee opened a door that I hadn't even seen, and the silhouette of a chained man stood before me. The sudden flood of light into the room gave me an immediate recollection of who dude was, and where I had met him. I couldn't believe that Supreme's cousin actually stood before me. This was truly a surprise, and my bright, smiling face reflected it.

I turned to Monty, and before I could question him about how he had come across Unique, he threw his arms wide and shrugged his shoulders. Smiling deviously, he held the chain and growling pit at bay as it fought to get to Unique. Picking up on the angry growls of the pit that Monty held, the other two dogs began to bark violently.

My brain was working in overdrive as I made my way into the tiny room and stared into Unique's battered face. Glaring back at me through defiant, unblinking eyes, he spat at my feet when I snatched the duct tape from his mouth. Laughing arrogantly, he snapped, "Apparently you bitches don't know who I am, but I'll let your stupidity pass this time! Unchain me, and as a favor I'll let everyone live, except your faggot ass!" he said, eyeing Rolee with a look of hatred.

The loud laughter that erupted around the room was contagious. Even Rolee had to chuckle at the arrogant outburst.

I had to admit that the New Yoker had heart. But heart or not, he couldn't have realized who he was dealing with. Locking eyes with him, I spoke in a cold, calculated tone, making sure to emphasize every word. "I know exactly who the fuck you are, Unique." Noticing the way his eyes narrowed when I said his name, I continued. "I guess you forgot who I am, though. But that's cool. Maybe the name Chez will jar your memory."

Recognition was immediately evident in his eyes, and although he didn't allow any fear to show, his words weren't as cocky as before. "Nah, money. I don't know any Chez. I got mad dough though. All you niggas got to do is let me go, and whatever you want is yours," he declared through swollen lips.

"Give me the keys to these cuffs!" I commanded over my shoulder, hearing the angry sighs behind me as I saw a sly grin creep to the corner of Unique's mouth. Receiving the key, I decided that although I wasn't going to free him completely, he would get more than they had given me years ago. Unsnapping one of his restraints, I gave him a fighting chance. Turning to walk away, I left one of his arms cuffed to a chain that was at least four feet long.

"Yo, where you going, son?" he loudly questioned with a trace of fear in his voice. "Take the other one off! I'm telling you, I got too much money, dog!"

Ignoring his pleas, I tossed the key back to Monty and walked out of the room. "Handle your business, lil' brah," were the only words I felt were necessary.

Showing his gold grill as he smiled his signature devilish grin, Monty waved his hand at E.J. Without a word being exchanged between them, E.J. released the first pit into the room. Attacking before the words, "Get 'em, boy!" were even out of his mouth, the pit lunged for Unique's chest with bared teeth.

I stood still with unblinking eyes, watching the dog tear chunks out of Unique's body.

The fight was hardly one-sided, because even with the pain he had to be experiencing, Unique fought the pit tooth and nail. Rolling around on the floor, the dog growled and whimpered while Unique screamed and grunted. The nigga was a fighter, and even though he bled profusely, he somehow managed to wrap the chain around the pit's neck.

Seeing the blood that covered the floor along with the fight taking place before them, the pits that Rolee and Monty held, pulled on their chains in an attempt to join the attack. Pawing the floor as they growled, foam escaped their mouths in anticipation.

Bending forward, Monty spoke to Dozier in a low tone that seemed to somewhat quiet his fury. Grabbing the clasp that held his chain in place, he released Dozier at the exact moment that Rolee unhooked the third pit. Watching as Dozier went straight for Unique's throat, Monty excitedly exclaimed, "That's my boy! He did exactly what I told his ass to do!" Yelling above Unique's loud, blood-curdling screams, Monty said, "Rolee, make sure you get this shit on tape, brah!"

Staring at the vicious scene before me with an expressionless look on my face, I concluded that he would soon be taking his last breath. The dogs were basically feasting on his exposed insides as it was. I'd had enough of this grotesque sight for one day. It was time to go. My woman and an escape from the cruelty of my daily existence awaited.

I leaned towards Monty, and spoke above the growls and screams. "I'm out, brah. Make me a copy of that tape, and grab all the nigga's jewelry for me. I think I'll send them and the tape to Supreme."

Momentarily taking his attention off of the slaughter, Monty chuckled. "Yeah, that shit will surely fuck him up. I got you. Enjoy yourself," he said, getting back to the show.

Shaking my head as I turned to walk away, it hit me that these niggas were too cold for them to be as sane as I had thought they were in the beginning. When I returned, I decided that I would get this shit over with once and for all. The more people that died, the less I could recall why.

Heading out of the abandoned house, all I knew was that somewhere along the way, my hatred had grown to dangerous proportions.

Hitting the Interstate, I actually felt rejuvenated. It seemed like the more distance I placed between myself and the city, the more clearly I was able to breathe. For the first time in my life, I-95 had become more than just a highway; it was my own personal escape route.

I lowered the volume on my newly installed system and I punched in the numbers to Toshia's phone. I balanced it between my ear and shoulder and reached for a Black and Mild while I listened to the phone ring. Just when I thought I'd be making a surprise entrance into DC, I heard my baby pick up.

"Hello," Toshia said in her calm, sexy manner.

"Hello back to you!" I teased, smiling at the excitement I knew my coming to Washington would bring her.

"Hey, baby! I miss you!" she purred in a syrupy tone.

"The feeling is mutual, but I miss you more!" Pausing to spark the Mild, I inhaled then added, "I'm on the highway, and I'll be in DC in about an hour."

"Stop playing, Chez! Are you serious?" she excitedly questioned.

"As serious as I can possibly be. In fact, when I get there, we're going on a shopping spree. I haven't bought a wardrobe yet, and I think you deserve a few nice things as well."

"Umm-hmm, I could definitely use a few nice things," she snickered excitedly.

"Yeah, I figured you would feel that way!" I chuckled. "I need you to do me a favor though. Take out three hundred grand, 'cause I didn't bring any money up this hot ass highway, alright?"

"Three hundred thousand?" she snapped in disbelief. "Baby, I know you're not going to spend that kind of money."

Laughing at her amazed tone, I replied, "No, I'm not going to spend it. We are! That's nothing though, mama. Stick with the kid, and you'll see that it gets greater later!"

"Baby, that's too much! We couldn't possibly spend--"

Cutting short any objections she had, I butted in. "Look, sweetheart. I gotta go, but I'll be there in another hour. I love you!" I said and ended the call.

I shook my head as I dropped the phone in my lap. It was funny to me that she was alarmed at the thought of spending such a large sum of money. Today would only be the beginning of our splurging. With the plans that I had in mind, our bank would increase drastically in the next few weeks.

After inhaling the smooth smoke from the Mild, I exhaled slowly, deciding that as soon as I returned, I would finally make my appearance in the city. It was time that all my enemies knew that I'd returned. I couldn't wait to see their faces when the nightmare began.

Toshia still hadn't gotten accustomed to being around such large sums of money. Counting out the three hundred thousand that Chez had instructed her to remove, she couldn't help comparing the money to a sea of green bills. Even now as she counted it, she couldn't imagine how it would be possible to spend such a large sum. However, if Chez said it was possible, she had no doubt that it could be done. Letting the thought pass, she made up her mind to enjoy the task.

More than any shopping trip, she planned to enjoy the company of her man. With Chez coming home, she excitedly realized that the deep itch inside her could finally be scratched. Anticipating what would take place between them, she pushed the bag filled with money to the side and headed to the waiting shower. After being apart for two weeks, she planned to look her best when he arrived.

Unlike the many lame women she knew who figured that the way to a man's heart was through his stomach, Toshia knew better. As far as she was concerned, the way to his heart was through his eyes. Fuck food! If she looked delicious enough, it was her that he would be eating.

Grinning smugly as she discarded her clothing, Toshia had no doubt that tonight it would be her that Chez had an appetite for.

Toshia had fallen in love with the big, pretty Navigator at first sight. The state of the art audio and video equipment outfitted throughout the truck only amplified her love for the vehicle.

"You like this joint?" I asked, fingering my new platinum and diamond chain with the iced out scorpion medallion.

Taking her eyes off the road, she replied, "Damn right I like it! For eighty thousand dollars, who wouldn't?" She pulled in front of Adrienne Furriers as instructed. "What are you getting out of there, boo?" she asked.

"You just sit tight and you'll see soon," I responded, getting out of the truck and heading inside the store. I already knew what I wanted, so I didn't plan to be there long.

"Excuse me. May I help you with anything, sir?" a short, well-dressed white gentleman asked, approaching me with a quick stride.

Noticing an attractive black female cut her approach to me short, with a look of disgust on her face at the apparent competitiveness from her male counterpart, I gave him a cold look. "Nah, you can't help me!" I spat. "Could I bother you for a moment, Ms.?" I asked, dismissing him and pointing to the female instead.

Moving towards me quickly, she blushed, yet snubbed her nose in a triumphant manner at her co-worker before asking, "What can I do for you, sir?"

Unable to control the smile that came to my features, I cleared my throat and said, "Show me your mink collection for men and women. Then, I would like to see your chinchillas for both as well."

"Follow me," she stated with a smile.

Looking at her newly purchased Cartier watch, Toshia wondered what could possibly be taking Chez so long. She was still in awe of the fact that he had actually spent thirteen thousand on it. That wasn't even counting what he had dropped on the huge diamond ring and matching bracelet. When it came down to spoiling a female, she had to admit that no one did it quite like Chez. In fact, he was the only man who had ever spoiled her, period.

Seeing him coming out of the store with two hands full of long garment bags, she examined them to see what he could have possibly bought when the back of the truck was already full of their earlier purchases.

Unable to decide between the two short, hooded minks and two chinchillas of the same style, I had just bought them all. Only with mine, I had bought a matching safari-style chinchilla hat. I placed the bags in the back of the truck, jumped in the passenger seat and said, "Let's go."

"What's in the bags, baby?" Toshia asked as she pulled off.

"You'll find out later," I replied, dismissing her question.

"I want to know now!" she said, frowning her face up in a cute little pout.

"Nope! I can't tell you. It will ruin the surprise." Turning up the music, I inwardly smiled at the look on her face. I had spent over 300 grand in one day, and I had no complaints. If anything, it felt good to spoil my lady after all she had done for me. Leaning back in the seat, I had to admit that I was happier right now than I had been in a long time.

I relaxed in the comfort of Toshia's embrace and stared into the burning embers of the fireplace as we discussed our future. What had started out as a private modeling session for her to flaunt her new furs, had turned into a long, sweet session of lovemaking. The sight of her body draped in fur, a thong and stiletto boots was more than I could handle. But as sexy as she is, Toshia would have had the same effect on me if she had been wearing fatigues and army boots.

"Baby, I really needed that," she sighed, wiping sweat from my brow. "When are you coming home for good, Chez? God knows, I need you here with me, boy!"

"Real soon," I said, staring into her dark, smoldering eyes. "Within the next couple of weeks, this shit will be all over with. I promise you, ma."

"I can't wait!" she exclaimed, hugging me tightly. Wrapping her thick, juicy legs around my waist, she asked, "Then what?"

I wiped a loose strand of hair out of her eye and kissed her gently. Breaking the kiss, I said, "If it's cool with you, when I return, we can move to Jamaica, build a big beautiful house by the ocean, and spend the remainder of our days just like this."

With excitement evident in her eyes, Toshia looked deep into mine. "Are you serious, baby? Can we really move to Jamaica?" she asked in disbelief.

Holding her stare, I sincerely stated, "I've never been more serious than I am at this moment."

"Oh, my God!" she yelled, and gave me a deep, hungry kiss. "If it's cool with me? Are you serious? The way I love you… boy, I would follow your ass to the end of the world!"

I loved her as well. If the end of the world was where ballers headed when the game was over, then that was exactly where we would go. Sliding further between her legs, I quickly found that Jamaica wasn't the only place to find paradise. The silken walls that gripped me were my definition of paradise at the moment.

"Yeah… baby! Right there!" Toshia whimpered in a deep, cracking voice. Swirling her hips, she groaned, "You have me so-o-o-o wet right now, boo!"

I cupped her shapely ass in my palms as I worked myself deeper into her soaked center, I made a silent promise that I would get my business over with quickly and return to her. Closing my eyes tightly as her spasming muscles gripped me, I realized that more than any other place, right here was where I belonged.

Chapter 15

Although Supreme hadn't been able to track Unique down in over a week of looking high and low, he was still in rare form as he stepped from the back of the Bentley.

Draped in a Roberto Cavalli dress with matching jewel-studded heels and a fur coat, Monya looked as beautiful as ever exiting the car behind him.

Expressionless, Supreme held a hand out to grasp Monya's as they headed towards the entrance. It was times like these that he needed a showpiece, and even though he had numerous women, Monya was the showstopper that easily solidified his position as the "King of the City." With Mann covering his front, while Tee and a team of bodyguards secured his back, Supreme personified royalty.

Smiling more for effect than any sense of happiness, Monya held onto his arm dutifully. She would have preferred to remain at home, than to have to come to a fake Players Ball where Supreme had more than likely fucked every female in attendance. Though she realized that she could never be so lucky, she couldn't help thinking that tonight would be the perfect opportunity for the feds to come and lock Supreme up, along with the countless hustlers in attendance who kissed his ass daily. However, it would never be anything more than a thought, because the truth of the matter, was that Supreme was way too sharp for that.

The loud music quickly assaulted their eardrums when they entered the ballroom. Heading through the huge crowd of partygoers, it seemed as if everyone attempted to get near them. Instead of acknowledging them, Supreme acted like none of them even existed as their entourage moved towards the VIP section. He felt that they were basically beneath him. If they served no purpose in increasing his riches, they truly served no purpose.

Seeing the way that Supreme treated people, Monya couldn't believe that he was the same man she had once loved. It had gotten to the point where she could hardly stand to be around him, much less love him. She often found herself comparing him to Chez. She knew that Chez would have never treated people in the same manner. He was respectful, but dangerous, and that was what placed him a step above the others.

Hearing her name called, Monya snapped out of her dream state.

Frowning, Supreme appeared to be agitated as he held out a chair for her to be seated. "Are you planning to stand up the rest of the night or what?" he snapped angrily.

"I'm sorry. Yes, I would like to sit," she replied, removing her coat and handing it to him. Taking her seat, she was oblivious to the stares of the people who already occupied their table.

Thinking that she could use a good slap, Supreme roughly pushed her chair up to the table. With all the things that he already had on his mind, he was hardly in the mood to be dealing with her antics. Between the losses he had taken in money, product and manpower, not to mention Unique's disappearance, the next whipping she made him give her would be brutal. Cutting his eyes evilly in her direction as he dropped down in his seat, Supreme decided that the time had come for Monya to be replaced.

As she sat in the VIP lounge, slowly sipping her champagne, Neeta observed Monya and Supreme's entrance. Through the use of boss game, she had conned Dresser into bringing her to the party. He was completely wrapped around her finger, and that's exactly how she planned to keep him.

Noticing the interaction between Monya and Supreme, she could tell that their relationship was far from happy. From the looks of all the ice that dripped from Monya's frame, it was apparent to her that even though the honeymoon seemed to be over, the relationship was still a profitable one.

Poking her lips out in a pout, Neeta couldn't believe that even though she had been in a relationship of sorts with Chez and Supreme, she still couldn't find one reason to hate Monya. In all truth, she was actually beautiful. Neeta seldom wasted her time worrying about others, but for some reason she felt sorry for Monya. With a maniac like Supreme for a man, it was more than likely that she was going through hell.

"You know you're the baddest chick in the house tonight, right?" Dresser whispered in Neeta's ear, getting her full attention. "And for the record, you're wearing the hell out of that Versace dress, ma."

She removed her eyes from Monya, and gave Dresser her award-winning smile. Blushing, she lightly pecked him on the cheek, and dismissed him just as quickly. Gazing around the room as she sipped from the champagne flute, she too realized that she was wearing the hell out of the strapless Versace original. He was definitely telling the truth, and after the long money he had dropped to drape her in the finest design, she had no problem with flaunting her million-dollar frame in it. Grinning smugly, she began to scheme and plot, because for her, the game never stopped. If she continued to have her way, Dresser would bow down completely, and real soon.

My Navigator led the caravan of luxury vehicles up the exit ramp into Petersburg. I had that Tupac pumping at the max level

I ain't a killer but don't push me

Revenge is like the sweetest joy next to getting pussy

Picture paragraphs unloaded, wise words being quoted

Peeped the weakness in the rap game and sewed it

Bow down, pray to God hoping that he's listening

Seeing niggas coming for me, to my diamonds, when they glistening.

The song was perfect for the way I was feeling, with Monty's Benz and his Lexus cruising directly behind me. Lavar followed Monty's whips in his dark green Cadillac DTS, while E.J. brought up the rear in his white on white STS. Twenty-inch rims adorned each whip's feet.

Twenty deep and packing enough heat to deal with any beef, we were a force to be reckoned with. If needed, we were more than ready to shut the party down.

Now, I was just ready to reach our destination. After five years of waiting for this, I was only moments away from making my dream a reality. The city would witness my return.

"You good over there, brah?" Monty asked, placing a package in my lap.

"Yeah, I'm cool, man." Lifting the package, I said, "I was just thinking, that's all."

"Well, that makes two of us," he stated, watching me as I shook the package he had given me.

"What's on your mind, lil' brah? And what the hell is in this box?" I questioned, unable to figure the shit out on my own.

"It's the jewelry and the tape you asked me to get from the nigga, Unique," Monty replied with a smirk. "Anyway, I was just wondering if you're sure you want to do it like this? Shit! As far as I'm concerned, we could always run up in that bitch masked up and get to flipping shit."

"Nah, it's got to be done this way. When their organization tumbles, everyone needs to know exactly who's responsible."

"I don't agree with you this time, Chez. You know I'm with you, but I'm not used to letting my enemies know that I'm coming," he argued.

Giving serious thought to his words, I couldn't help having a few doubts myself. Maybe this wasn't the best move after all, but my pride was at stake, and I had to save face.

Glancing up ahead, I was greeted by the sight of traffic and people everywhere. The crowd that stood in a line that seemed to be endless, clearly indicated to me and my entourage that we had arrived at our destination. Disregarding any doubts that may have been lingering before, I set my mind upon the one thing that had kept me focused throughout the years. Revenge was what I had lived for, and now it was time for the games to begin.

Bored to death, Monya turned up her third glass of Cristal. Spinning around to face Supreme, who was deep in conversation with one of his flunkies, she slurred, "I'm going to the bathroom."

Giving her a cold look as she stood, his only response was a slight grunt. Returning his attention back to the conversation he had been having, he turned his back to Monya and said, "My bad, man. She doesn't know any better. You know how silly bitches can be sometimes."

Rooted to her spot, Monya couldn't believe her ears. Supreme had never disrespected her in front of others. Undecided as to whether she wanted to cry or scream obscenities, she instead turned and walked away. Biting her lip in frustration as she calmly moved through the crowd, she made up her mind to show Supreme that she wasn't a silly bitch by far. Little did he know, his blatant show of disrespect had just set the wheels of destruction in motion. Determined now more than ever to make him pay, her stride quickened. Thanks to his stupidity, her direction was suddenly much clearer.

Neeta caught the whole episode that had taken place between Monya and Supreme, and it was clear that he had no regard for who may have witnessed it. He was cold hearted and inconsiderate, and she found it hard to believe that at one time she too had been crazy about him. Frowning at the thought, it dawned on her that other than some good dick and the financial support he was able to contribute, Supreme wasn't shit. One thing she didn't doubt, was that before it was over, his snake ass would get his.

Inwardly grinning at her last thought, she realized that like Supreme, she too had done her share of snake shit. Figuring that she would also one day have to pay for her deceitful ways, she hoped that her payday would arrive much later. Right now, every facet of her life was going just right, and she planned to keep having it her way.

Smiling wickedly, Neeta began to gyrate her body sexily in her seat. Her song was on, and for the moment, that's all that mattered.

We exited our vehicles and began to make our way through the crowded hotel entrance. Our crew was thick, and we were shining. Catching the reflection of Monty and myself in the mirrored entrance, it was easy to understand why the crowd openly gawked as we approached. "Ooh's and aah's" echoed around us.

However, along with all the admiring glances we received, there were even more hating stares thrown our way. I couldn't have cared less one way or the other, being that I was here for more important reasons than any of them could have begun to understand.

The hoods of our coats covered our faces, making it impossible to distinguish our identities. Not to mention the fact that our gear, by far, confirmed that we were the flyest niggas in the house. Then, to fuel their hatred even more, our whole crew was just as dipped as Monty and myself.

Arrogant and worthy of all the hungry looks the women were tossing my way, I knew that I was a sight for sore eyes. Draped in a silver and black Versace silk shirt, black silk Versace pants, and a pair of gray and black snake skin Versace boots with gold emblems on the sides, I was killing the game. I wore my short black and gray hooded chinchilla open so that the platinum and diamond chain and iced out scorpion medallion were in clear view. Other than my diamond bracelet and Patek Phillipe watch, a two-carat princess cut earring and Cartier frames completed my ensemble.

Monty wore royal blue and white Versace. His shirt, pants and boots were a reflection of my own, but the hooded white mink he wore placed him in a class by himself. Versace frames covered his eyes, and the ice covering the Jesus piece that swung from his neck was blinding.

Proud of the picture that we presented, I quickened my steps, suddenly in a hurry to enter the ballroom. We were killing the competition hands down, and as soon as the the doors opened and the crowd saw us, the immediate stares we received were proof.

Monya had just finished using the bathroom when two scantily dressed females entered. The loud chatter that accompanied them was instantly annoying to her. The even louder sucking sound she made as she rolled her eyes in their direction let them know it. Locking her eyes with them through the mirror, she continued washing her hands with a look of disgust etched on her features.

Cutting their eyes at one another the two girls dismissed her with a wave of their hands and even louder giggles, as they continued their conversation. "Girl, did you see how fly those niggas were that just stepped up in here?" one of them excitedly questioned.

"Hello!" the other yelled, even more excited. High-fiving her girl as they approached the sink near Monya, she exclaimed, "Bitch, you already know I was on them! They were all fly as hell, but did you see the two who were rocking the hoods?"

"Did I?" the taller of the two stated, throwing her head back for effect. "Girl, when they pulled those hoods off, I nearly came all over myself!" she informed with a fake groan.

Applying another coat of lip-gloss and a dab of perfume, Monya mumbled, "Silly ass bitches!" under her breath as she turned to leave. Almost to the door, she heard one of them mention a name that stopped her in her tracks.

"I hear you, ho. I've got to admit that the sight of Chez's ass in that chinchilla with all that ice on has my pussy dripping too. Umph! Umph! Umph! He's too damn fine! Girl, I want some of that!"

"I know, girl. Shit! I want some too, but the way they rolled up in here grillin', it definitely doesn't look like pussy is their first priority. Now that he's home, he's more than likely on a mission."

Pouting, the shorter female said, "I heard that he has a beef with Supreme and them. I only hope that he lives long enough to let me taste some of that thing," she giggled, giving her girl a pound.

Leaning against the wall for support, Monya mumbled, "Oh... my... God!" She couldn't believe that Chez was actually there. After being with him for twelve years, she should have known that he would pick an event like this to make his entrance. There was no doubt in her mind that he wouldn't rest until he had evened the score with Supreme and everyone else who had violated him.

Nervous at the thought of seeing him again, Monya figured that it was either now or never. At all costs, she needed to find a way to make contact with him before it was too late.

Pausing in his conversation due to the sounds of a commotion taking place on the dance floor, Dresser calmly peered into the crowd. Although it was entirely too packed to see through the crowded club, he was aware that whatever was taking place had to be getting closer. The parting sea of bodies on the lower level gave him an indication that something serious was in the air.

The sudden change of sound in the ballroom caused Neeta to stand up. She observed a large group of men parading through the aisles. She couldn't make out any of their faces, but the expensive furs and sparkling jewels they wore, more than proved to her that they were official. She was curious as to who they may be, and such a blatant show of wealth immediately piqued her interest.

Excited at the thought of snagging another baller as strapped as Dresser, she strained her eyes for a better look. Raising up on tiptoes to see above the crowd, her eyes suddenly grew wide as she felt her heart rate increase drastically. She blinked, and hoped that when her eyes reopened, the picture would be different. When they opened she was treated to the same view.

Dropping back down in her seat, Neeta was in a state of shock, and the only question that ran through her mind was, How did Chez get out?

I was amped as we made our way through the crowd. Returning to my city in such splendor was more exhilarating than I had ever dreamed. However, with every step I took, I realized that the stakes were getting higher and higher. The jewelry and videotape that weighed heavily inside my pocket proved that I played for keeps, so I wasn't concerned.

Scanning the crowd as I passed, I glimpsed numerous hustlers from my hood throwing up 3rd Ward signs. Their acknowledgements let me know that even though I traveled with twenty soldiers from Richmond, I was surrounded by my own people as well. The show of strength alone gave me that extra dose of cockiness I needed, and I knew that whatever moves I decided to make, they would back me up.

Rolling up in the VIP section with my crew in tow, I cut my eyes in the direction of my enemies. The surprised looks that reflected back at me registered a mixture of shock and fear. Winking my eye in their direction, our entourage headed to the bar. The looks I saw on Supreme, Neeta and Dresser's faces were just what I had expected. Just like I predicted, my face was one that they had never planned to see again. How wrong they had been! I thought as I took a seat at the bar.

I waved the bartender over and informed him that we wanted every bottle of champagne that he had. I pulled out a huge knot of bills and stuffed a few C-notes in his shirt pocket. Before he could protest, I said, "Send five bottles to that table over there," referring to the one that my enemies occupied. "Oh, and just in case they refuse, we're not taking 'no' for an answer!"

"I got you!" He smiled and walked off to fill my order.

"What the hell was that about?" Monty snapped, eyeing me foolishly. "How you gonna roll up in here buying them motherfuckers champagne after what they did to you, brah?"

I shook my head at the anger I witnessed in Monty's eyes. I knew that he probably thought I was losing my mind. However, I knew exactly what I was doing. "Relax, brah. Let me do this my way, alright? There's a method to my madness, believe me!"

Swiveling around on the barstool to face my enemies with a cool, calm look on my face, I smiled inwardly. I knew that they were wracking their brains in an attempt to figure out what was going through my head, and wondering when I would strike. The fun part was that they were now at my mercy. The only thing was, mercy was one thing I no longer had.

Chapter 16

From where she stood hidden within the crowd, Monya could see Chez clearly. She found it hard to believe that he was actually this close. Staring through unblinking eyes, she had to admit that he looked even better to her now, than before. Caught up in the sight before her, she decided that if she planned to make contact with him, this was the time to do so. Supreme would surely be searching for her now that Chez had arrived, so she knew that she needed to hurry. The last thing she needed was to make him suspicious.

Moving quickly, she removed a pen from her purse and wrote down her cell phone number. "Please call! Very important! Monya." was all she could think to scribble before folding the paper in a crude fashion.

Nervously searching the sea of faces around her for someone trustworthy to deliver the note, she saw someone who fit the bill. She waved for her cousin, Pierre, as she glanced in the direction of the VIP room to make sure that Supreme was still seated, she attempted to calm her nerves.

Pierre gave her a hug and said, "I see you're looking as beautiful as ever tonight, cuz."

Returning the embrace, Monya got straight to the point, figuring that this wasn't the time for small talk. "I need your help, cuz." She placed the folded paper in his hand. "I don't have time to explain, but I need you to deliver this to Chez at the bar. Tell him that whatever he's planning to do, please hold off until he talks to me, Pierre."

Seeing the serious look on her face, Pierre said, "You know you owe me big for this one, girl. But you know I got you, right?" Turning to walk away, he winked his eye and shot her a grin.

Watching her cousin as he headed towards the bar, Monya bit her lip nervously. After what she had done to him, she couldn't quite say how he would react to her message, but she just hoped he wouldn't disregard it all together. Even though she had failed to hold him down when he needed her, in the hopes of making things right, she planned to turn over Supreme's riches to him. *Maybe if I play my cards right, he would even take me back*, she thought, watching him in a daze.

Sipping from my own bottle of Cris, I watched the gorgeous females who shamelessly paraded around us. Although they were delicious eye candy, my real attention was focused on Monty's words.

"Fuck playing games with these motherfuckers! Let's deal with them tonight!"

Listening to his fiery words, but failing to respond, I couldn't help the smile that crept upon my face. He was ready for war, but if he allowed me to work my hand, he would see that we were on the same page. Tired of his ranting, I cut him off in mid-sentence. "Relax nigga! It's going down tonight. Alright?"

Smiling, he replied, "That's more like it then. Now, how about you let me in on how it's going down, brah?"

I cut my eyes in the direction of Supreme's table. "If I know these coward motherfuckers like I think I do, any minute now they're gonna start leaving." Turning back around to face Monty, I said, "When they leave, I need you to have them tailed. Once we know where they lay their heads, we handle our business. Niggas are dying tonight, lil' brah."

"Chez! What's up, my nigga?" Pierre casually stated, sliding up beside me at the bar.

"Ain't shit," I replied, giving him a pound. "How's life been treating you though?"

"You know me, fam. I'm just trying to survive," he stated as he slid Monya's note across the bar. "I'm just the messenger, man," he added.

I glanced at the folded piece of paper in front of me, then picked it up and quickly read the contents. I refolded it and placed it in my pocket. I allowed my eyes to do a 360-degree sweep of the club. Locking eyes with the individual I had sought out, I stared at her with an expressionless look on my face.

Monya was just as beautiful as I had remembered. Yet, her beauty had no relevance, because regardless of how good she looked, she was still the enemy. As much as I hated to think of her as such, nothing would change her status. However, due to her being here with Supreme, my plans for his demise, at least as far as tonight was concerned, had changed. He would live another day, because the last thing I wanted to do was jeopardize the life of my daughter's mother.

Taking it from there, Monty leaned towards Rolee and whispered something in his ear. Cutting his eyes in their direction, Rolee drained his drink and stood. Three more members of their crew did the same. Watching them leave the club, Monty said, "They're on it, brah."

Placing my attention back on Supreme, I reflected on the fact that although he would get away from me tonight, Dresser and Neeta wouldn't be so lucky. I reached inside my coat for Unique's jewelry and the videotape. I decided to just leave it with Dresser for safekeeping. When they found his body, Supreme would also have a chance to find out what happened to his cousin.

Regardless of how hard Neeta tried to keep from staring in Chez's direction as they made their way out of the club, she just couldn't help herself. With seemingly no control over her eyes, she found herself staring into his handsome face. In sort of a dream state, she thought he looked really good. Even with all the paid, fly niggas in attendance, no one at the Players Ball could touch him in her eyes. Nevertheless, it didn't matter how good he looked to her, because she knew that sharing in his splendor was the one thing she would never do again. Any bridge that may have led back into his life had been burned long ago.

Breaking eye contact as she exited the club, she nervously wondered what he planned to do about her double cross. It wasn't like him to let anything go, and she was hardly going to believe that his years away had changed him that much. She stepped off the curb into the 740 Beamer that awaited them. She knew that she wouldn't have long to wonder what Chez had in store. He would be coming after them; she had no doubt about that.

Never one to let a nigga see him sweat, Supreme sat with his legs crossed, and drank Chez's complimentary champagne as he watched his arch enemy at the bar. Chez posed a serious threat to his rule in the city, and that wasn't something he took lightly. Although he presented a calm front for everyone who knew their history, inside he was nervously thinking of ways to get rid of Chez once and for all.

Deciding that in the morning he would beef up security around himself and their estate, Supreme smiled. He looked around at the bodyguards who stood at their posts with ice glares, and concluded that it would take an army to get at him. In his mind, he had placed himself on a major pedestal, and he truly felt untouchable. Even Monya, who at one time belonged to Chez, was now faithfully by his side for all to see. The more he thought about what he now possessed, the less he cared about the threat Chez's return represented.

He leaned towards Monya and kissed her lingeringly for everyone to see. Breaking their kiss, he asked, "You ready to blow this joint, baby?"

Seething inside at the fake show of affection Supreme had put on for Chez's benefit, Monya wanted to explode. But instead of showing her true feelings, she kept her composure and gave him the phoniest smile she could muster. "Whenever you're ready, I'm ready, boo."

Supreme stood and reached for Monya's hand. He helped her to her feet and placed her fur coat over her shoulders. Grabbing his own coat, Supreme motioned for his bodyguards and made his way through the VIP with Monya in tow.

Even though I had seen every move he'd made, I was far from impressed. To be perfectly honest, I was more amused than anything. He may have felt that he had done something cute, but I knew that the last laugh would belong to me.

Catching their eyes as they walked by, I winked slyly and raised my bottle of Cris in a mock toast. Dismissing them just as quickly as I had acknowledged their presence, I turned towards Monty and saw that he was ending a call.

"Yo, Rolee just got at me," he said, placing the phone back in his pocket. "The two of them went to a house in Richmond. I've got the address, and I gave the order for no one to move on them until we arrive," he informed in an anxious tone.

"Let's not keep them waiting," I replied, standing up. I was more than ready to get at Dresser and Neeta. They were snakes, and it wasn't surprising to me that they were seeing each other. At least with the present arrangement, I would be able to deal with them together.

I picked up my pace, and Monty's steps quickened as well. There was no time to waste, because we were both in a hurry to draw first blood.

A short while later, we pulled up beside Rolee and the others. He exited his vehicle and immediately pointed in the direction of a large, tri-level gray house. Although they weren't expecting our arrival, I still scanned the layout of the house in order to put together the perfect plan that would accomplish my goals.

I removed my coat and jewelry and laid them in the front seat. Monty did the same. He placed a Glock 9-mm in my hand with an extra clip, and jacked a round into the chamber of his own Glock. "You ready to go?" he asked.

Nodding my head in the affirmative, I opened the door, allowing the cold air to rush into the warm truck. Sprinting in a low, crouching manner across the frozen grass, we made it to the back of the house without alarming barks from the neighborhood dogs. My adrenaline was pumping hard.

The weight of the jewelry and videotape inside my jacket was a silent reminder of just how violent and cold the niggas around me were. They were here to assist me in my revenge, and regardless of the feelings I'd once harbored for Neeta and Dresser, I was here to make them pay. Nothing would stop me from accomplishing my task.

I faced Monty in the darkness, and gave the signal that it was a go. The crashing sound that followed was loud and thunderous as the back door exploded inward. Moving with lightening speed, we entered the house and ran towards the candlelit bedroom.

Dresser and Neeta were immersed in the heated sudsy water of the whirlpool, as Mariah Carey soothed them with her beautiful rendition of "Butterfly". The numerous candles that lit the bathroom gave it a romantic setting, but it was the feel of her body gliding slowly up and down on his own that made Dresser forget his earlier worries. The euphoric feeling of her center and the sweet kisses she rained all over his face and neck between moans and pleasurable whimpers gave him an invincible feeling.

She tossed her head back as she rode Dresser in the way that she knew drove him mad. Neeta slammed herself down on him hard and fast. The loud clapping sound that their flesh made when they collided was a turn on to her. Biting down on her lip, she closed her eyes tightly at the feel of an approaching orgasm.

"Ka-Boom!"

The sound resonated throughout the house, halting their movements. Both of their eyes were suddenly wide open. The fear of the unknown could be seen within them.

Pushing Neeta off of him and into the sudsy water, Dresser jumped out of the whirlpool. Running, he slipped and fell face-first on the black marble tile with a loud thump. Nervously scurrying back to his feet, he continued his mad dash to the bedroom. He realized that if he planned to make it through the night, he would have to reach the .45 Smith and Wesson that lay on the dresser.

The heavy footfalls Dresser heard nearing the closed door indicated that more than one person was headed his way. His time was limited if he didn't reach his weapon soon. Moving with the speed of a leopard, he dove across the bed at the exact moment the bedroom door flew open with an ear-shattering force. Only inches away from the chrome automatic, he heard the unmistakable voice that had haunted many of his dreams through the years.

"Touch it, and I'll empty this whole clip in your ass, nigga!" Chez hissed in a cold, deadly tone that left no doubt as to his intentions.

With his fingers lingering only inches away from the .45, Dresser turned in the direction of his old friend. At the sight of Chez standing in the doorway with a 9-mm trained on him, the only thought that came to mind was, It had to come down to this sooner or later. Figuring that he was going to die anyway, he decided that if he had to go, he might as well try and take someone along for the ride. Suddenly smiling at the circumstances he now found himself in, Dresser began to chuckle. Maintaining eye contact, his eyes narrowed, giving him a sinister appearance. Without warning or regret, he reached for the weapon.

Bullet after bullet tore into Dresser's upper torso, spraying blood and chunks of his flesh all over the sheets and wall as they exited. As promised, Chez emptied the clip into him. The loud sound of the 9-mm and the shrill screams from Neeta filled the room.

Naked and shivering, Neeta cowered in the corner of the bathroom. Tears streamed down her face as she grieved; not for Dresser, but for the death she knew awaited her once he no longer breathed. Hearing footsteps approaching, she looked up into the face that now represented nothing more than her demise. Chez was the Grim Reaper, and the evil look on his face said it all. Her time had arrived.

I allowed my gaze to momentarily linger on Neeta's luscious frame. I felt an old sexual urge that I thought had ceased to exist long ago. Her sweet, brown frame hadn't lost a single drop of the allure I had once found so tempting. After all the years that I had been away, she still presented a picture of utter perfection. Second-guessing my original plan, I felt that if I were to put a bullet into such perfection, I wouldn't be able to live with myself.

Neeta hugged herself tightly, as if bracing herself for the inevitable bullets. She opened her eyes and a look of surprise crossed her face, when the burning look in Chez's eyes was the only thing that bore into her body. Drawing strength from his apparent appraisal, she began to speak in a pleading, trembling voice in hopes of saving her life. "Baby, plea... please... don't hurt me! I... I know... I know I fucked up, but you were... always on my mind... no matter what."

I lowered the gun a little, and this seemed to give her confidence. She began to speak even faster. "Chez, we've been through too much. I know you haven't forgotten how good we once were together," she stated desperately. "I still love you, Chez, and not even you can execute the woman who loves you."

"You're right," I sighed, dropping the arm that held the Glock to my side. "I can't kill you, ma."

By the sudden gleam I noticed in her eyes, I could tell that once again, she felt as though she had gotten her way. Regardless of who she crossed and hurt in the process, she never expected to receive any punishment for her actions. Shaking my head in disgust, I could no longer understand what I had seen in her in the first place.

Turning to walk out of the bathroom, I said the words that I knew would wipe the gleam out of her eyes and make her heart skip a beat. "I may not be able to kill you, but my little brother will!" Eyeing Monty as I walked past him, I said, "Kill that bitch, Brah!"

I tossed the jewelry and videotape on Dresser's prone body as I strolled through the room. The last words I heard from Neeta were, "No! Please don't do this! Please! I'll do anything, Chez!"

As I entered the hallway, her pleas were silenced by the loud weapon that erupted. Picking up my pace, I recalled the words I had said to her on a sandy beach, years before. I asked her never to cross me. Now, it was evident that she hadn't taken me seriously. Look what happened.

Grinning as I walked out into the cold night, I mumbled, "You should have listened, Neeta!"

It was a new day, and I hadn't slept in over twenty-four hours. After watching the sun come up, I had spent the rest of the morning lying in bed, contemplating whether I should use the number Monya had given me. What I couldn't get out of my head was why she needed to talk to me now. After all this time and no word whatsoever as to how she and my daughter were doing, what could she possibly want with me?

Rubbing my eyes, I knew that I needed some rest, but at the moment I had too much on my mind to even think that sleep would be possible. The words, Please call! Very important! Jumped out at me as I peered at Monya's message. Even though a part of me said to tear the note up, another part said that because of all the years she did stand by me, she deserved to at least be heard, if nothing else.

I reached for the phone and reluctantly began to dial the number on the paper. Listening to the ringing phone, I had mixed feelings, but I had already made up my mind to hear her out.

Snapping to attention at the sound of the phone being picked up, I immediately heard Monya's sleep-filled voice. "Hello."

Wanting to hang up, I found myself unable to do so. Instead, I cleared my throat and spoke in an unsure voice. "I got your message..."

Chapter 17

Monya was floating on cloud nine with a permanent smile plastered on her face. Ever since her earlier conversation with Chez, she had been more exhilarated than she had been in years. Though the beginning of their conversation had been somewhat awkward, they had gotten past it. Finding common ground in their daughter, Monya was able to break through Chez's defenses. Chanae was truly the bright spot in each of their lives. Therefore, Monya knew that whatever transpired between them, their daughter would always be the factor that had the power to bridge any gaps.

Although she could have said what she needed to say over the phone, Monya chose to use her information as a means of luring him into a meeting. Setting up a time and place for their rendezvous, she found herself excited to no end at the mere thought of being in his presence.

Twirling her long, wavy hair around a finger, she could only imagine what it would be like to make love to the man who was her first for everything that made her the woman she now was. Shivering at the thought of being with Chez again, she closed her eyes tightly and shook her head in an attempt to clear her mind.

She carefully applied her berry lip-gloss, pressing her lips tightly together to smear it properly. She shook out her long, curly mane, and stared in the mirror at the completed package. She decided that she presented a picture of perfection.

Turning to the side, she smiled mischievously at the sight of the slit in her short Prada dress. Running her hands over the contours of her thick frame, she found that the slightest move she made raised the slit just enough to give a clear view of her upper thigh and ass. With her abundant assets on display, she figured that it would be virtually impossible for Chez to resist her. Disregarding any thoughts of failure, she was ready to depart for their rendezvous.

Reaching for her Prada purse and shades, she grabbed her Ferrari keys off the dresser and headed out the door. On a mission, the only thing she had on her mind was regaining what she felt belonged to her. Chez.

Pacing back and forth through his office, Supreme resembled a caged animal. In an outraged state, a caged animal is exactly what he felt like at that moment. Though he had tried to play down the threat of Chez's homecoming, it was now obvious that he presented a major problem. After what he had stumbled across earlier, it was clear that Chez had to be dealt with soon.

Dresser and Neeta had been found in pools of their own blood. It was only when the jewelry belonging to Unique, and the videotape had been recovered, that the true damage had been done to Supreme. Unique was family, and that, to Supreme, was the ultimate act of war. Neeta and Dresser had meant nothing to him. Therefore, they had been expendable in his eyes. If not for the fact that Dresser still owed an outstanding bill on 50 kilos, not even a second thought would have been spared on him. He could and would be easily replaced. Neeta, on the other hand, had already been dead as far as he was concerned. Her usefulness had run its course a long time ago.

However, Chez would have to pay in the worst way for what had been done to Unique. With traces of tears in his eyes, he reached for the AR-15 with the extended clip that lay on his desk. He pressed a button on his conference phone, and paced the room with his weapon cradled in his arms as the sound of a voice came through the intercom.

"Who this?" Mann snapped.

"Yo, I don't care how many people you have to put on his trail, but I'm placing a million dollar reward on Chez's head. I want him bad, son! And Mann, I expect some results on this shit ASAP!"

"I'm on it, Supreme. Let me spread the word, and the reward will make niggas move. I'm out, cuz!"

Dropping down in his chair with the assault rifle across his lap, Supreme pressed the remote and glared at the television screen. Watching the dogs eating his cousin for the third time, he couldn't control the tears that flowed from his eyes. The scene before him broke his heart, yet he forced himself to watch it again, so that he would never forget the pain his cousin had suffered. The same pain times ten would belong to Chez. That was the promise that he made to himself. This time, he planned to make sure that Chez would never be able to return.

I had second thoughts about meeting with Monya, but I decided to follow through with the meeting as scheduled. This would more than likely be the last time we saw each other, since I was leaving the country after I dealt with Supreme. I figured that after all the years we had shared together, closure was necessary.

Cutting through traffic, I made a detour from my planned path, into the parking lot of a convenience store. I exited the truck and dashed inside.

Glancing down at my diamond encrusted watch to gauge the time, it seemed as if the line ahead was moving at a snail's pace. Then again, maybe I just felt that way because I was in a hurry.

Looking up, I was pleasantly surprised when my eyes locked upon those of a chocolate sister who was beautiful to say the least. The mixture of surprised disbelief that I saw reflected in her eyes as she stared back at me made me wonder whether we had met before. I couldn't quite put my finger on it, but for some reason she looked familiar.

Breaking out in a smile, she revealed some of the most perfect, pearly-white teeth I had ever seen. Placing her hands on a set of deliciously wide hips, she said, "We meet again!" Opening her arms wide in invitation, she blushed, highlighting her cute little dimples. "Boy, you better give me a hug!"

Not one to turn down a chance at holding a beautiful woman, I quickly stepped into her embrace. Feeling the softness of her body pressed firmly against my own, I couldn't stop my mind from screaming, Who is this woman?

She released her hold on me, stepped back, and stated, "You're still looking real good, Chez." Shaking her head, she stared at me intensely and remarked, "This meeting was meant to be, because you've been on my mind a whole lot lately."

Listening to her speak, I wracked my brain trying to remember where I knew her from. Appraising her as she stood before me, I couldn't help but think that someone as fine as her should have been easy to remember. Snapping out of my reverie at the sudden seriousness I saw on her face, I gave her my undivided attention.

Clasping her hands in front of her breasts in a prayer-like fashion, she said, "God is good, Chez. He has placed you here at this moment to receive the message he gave me just for you."

She reached for my hands and grasped them tightly as she stared into my eyes. Holding the stare as if it were my soul she looked into, instead of my eyes alone, she began to speak again. "Our Father says to forgive all those who have sinned against you. A new and better path lies ahead of you, Chez. This path will bring you all the happiness that your life has lacked up to this point. But, any detour from it will only lead to destruction."

Snatching my hands out of her grasp, I found this whole situation to be creepy as hell. I hadn't come here to hear any religious premonitions, and the thing that ate at me the most was that her words were on point.

"Well, as I said before, it's been good seeing you again," she said, smiling as she stepped back with a look of understanding in her eyes. Turning to leave, she sincerely remarked, "It's your destiny, Chez. Be careful."

Unable to take my eyes off her as I reached the counter and paid for my cigarettes, I quickly exited the store. I still had no idea who the hell she was, but the white on white Benz that pulled out into traffic with "MIA 1" on the license plate immediately jarred my memory. Standing with my mouth wide open, I couldn't believe how Mia had changed. She was a far cry from the Mia I recalled from six years before. Grinning as I headed to my truck, I couldn't help thinking of the old Mia who loved tight clothes, had bomb head, and wore a lot of jewelry.

Jumping in the truck, her words ran through my mind: Our Father says to forgive all those who have sinned against you. A new and better path lies ahead of you. For some reason, her words left me with an uneasy feeling. I couldn't help thinking that maybe I should take heed of her warning.

Disregarding the thought, I turned my music up and put the truck in drive. I had somewhere I needed to be, and I was running late.

Toshia was ecstatic at the news she had just received. The symptoms of the last few weeks had alerted her to a possible pregnancy, and she had finally scheduled a visit with her personal physician. After a brief checkup, he confirmed that she was carrying a child.

Upon reaching the car, she found herself unable to pull off. The excitement she was experiencing at the mere thought of carrying a child-Chez's child-was beyond any other feeling she had ever known. The knowledge of how happy he would be once he found out, only increased the brightness of her smile. What made the news even more beautiful was that the new life they had already planned would only be enhanced by the birth of their first child.

She rummaged through her purse in search of her cell phone, but changed her mind. She placed the purse back in the passenger seat, deciding that news of this magnitude must be told in person. She rubbed her belly with a pleased look on her face, and whispered, "We'll just have to tell Daddy about you when he comes home."

As she pulled out into traffic, for once, Toshia felt like everything was going right in her life. Now that it was, she just hoped that nothing would come along to destroy her happiness.

Mann had a bad feeling in his gut as he oversaw the increase of security around Supreme's estate. From the moment he'd seen Chez walk into the club, there had been no doubt in his mind who was responsible for all of their recent misfortunes. Just when it seemed like they were on top of the world, the devil himself returned to bring death and destruction.

Finding Neeta and Dresser's bodies, along with the videotape of Unique's murder only served to strengthen Mann's belief that Chez was on a mission. Never one to be scared, he still found himself apprehensive at the realization that for Chez to have killed the woman he had once loved, and his childhood friend, he wouldn't have a problem with exacting revenge on anyone else. Chez was even more out of control now than he was in the past, and the thought didn't sit too well with Mann.

Staring around him at the twenty or so members of their crew, who all carried high-power assault rifles, Mann concluded that they were very necessary at this point. Strapped with two 10-mm handguns and a Mac-11 submachine gun himself, he wasn't about to take any chances with his own life either. When it was all said and done, the name of the game was self-preservation, and that was exactly how he planned to play it.

He retrieved his phone from his coat pocket and he dialed Supreme's cell phone to report that news of the reward on Chez's head had been spread, and the security had been beefed up as ordered. Even though precautions had been put into place, Mann couldn't help thinking that no amount of security would keep Chez from reaching whatever target he had in mind.

As I pulled into the Marriott parking lot, I noticed a black on black Ferrari whipping into a parking space up ahead. Recalling the conversation I had with my young homie in the pen, it was obvious that Monya had arrived only seconds before me. Grabbing the first parking space I saw, I decided to watch her and see what she did. Her entrance would surely be grand, but it wasn't her entrance that interested me. I didn't trust her, so from behind the tint on the

Navigator windows, I gauged her moves.

Monya parked and removed her mirrored compact from the Prada bag in the passenger seat, and then checked her flawless appearance. Smiling at the perfection she saw reflected back at her, she was ready for action. She sprayed a dab of Curve on her for the hell of it and she exited the car in a hurry. Her open-toed Gucci heels loudly clicked on the concrete as she rushed towards the hotel. Tossing her long, windblown hair out of her eyes, she checked the time on the Oyster Rolex she wore. She picked up her pace and hoped that the energy she was putting into her little ploy to reclaim Chez wouldn't be in vain. Refusing to believe that he could actually turn her away after all they had been through, she decided that it wasn't possible that he didn't want her as much as she did him.

Watching her every move and gesture, I couldn't help grinning. Still as fly and beautiful as she was years before, it was apparent that she hadn't changed one bit. It was true that she was stunning, but too much had changed between the two of us for this meeting to be anything other than business. The past, and whatever I felt for her was just that… the past.

Deciding that nothing would get accomplished by just sittingt here, I grabbed my gun from between the seat and exited the truck. I looked around as I made my way to the hotel entrance. I was aware that the meeting itself could possibly be an ambush. Gripping the Colt.45 that sat hidden inside my Avirex pocket, my finger coiled around the trigger in case I needed to make a quick retreat. I hoped that Monya hadn't stooped to the level where she actually wanted me dead, but if by chance it was that type of party, I would make sure to stay alive long enough to make sure that her pretty ass died as well. Not even my promise to Doc would save her life at that point. His baby girl and my daughter's mother would cease to exist.

I noticed the flirtatious smile of the cute desk clerk as I made my way through the lobby. I returned her smile and winked, as I continued on my course towards the elevators. Reaching an empty elevator and boarding it, I was on my floor, and standing at the door in no time flat. I paused before I placed the key card in the slot. I knew that Monya was already in the room, as I had left a key for her at the front desk. Sighing, I had no idea what to expect from her when I entered. I slid the card through the slot, and pushed the door wide open. I was about to find out.

Monya smiled as I entered the room. Nervously saying, "Hello," she leaned back into the plush couch, allowing the slit in her skirt to rise further up her already exposed thighs.

"What's up, Red?" I flatly replied as my eyes quickly took in the view of her thick, red thighs, and a portion of her ass through the slit in her skirt. At this point, I had an idea of what she was really here for, and I hoped she wasn't foolish enough to think that I would fall for her ploy. Averting my eyes, I headed in the direction of the bar. "What you drinking on?" I questioned over my shoulder, thinking that this little meeting she had devised would be over much quicker than she thought.

"Umm… I'll take whatever you're having," she replied in a nervous, whispery tone. Clearing her throat, she began to rake her fingers through her long curls in an uneasy manner.

After drinking my first shot of Hennessey, I made another drink for both of us, handed Monya hers and took a seat on the table directly in front of her. I could tell that my close proximity to her was unnerving her by the way that her large nipples began to harden, the rapid rising and falling of her chest was evident through the thin material of her dress. Noticing the way her eyes strayed around the room as she sipped her drink, I got straight to the point. "What is it that you needed to see me about, Monya?"

Swallowing the remainder of her drink, she exhaled lightly and ran her manicured hand around the rim of her glass. Raising her eyes to meet mine, she began to speak in a cracking voice. "Wh… what I'm about to say is hard, and I'm sure that you're not trying to really hear it, but please hear me out," she said with pleading eyes.

I sipped my drink with an expressionless look and nodded my head for her to continue. The only thing she wasn't aware of was no matter what she said or how sincere she said it, nothing would change how I viewed her. My heart was cold, and she was nothing more than the woman who had brought my daughter into the world.

"Well… first off… I'm sorry, Chez. I really am. I know that I could never take back what I've done, but I want to make it right."

Make it right? I thought, narrowing my eyes as an angry tide began to roll over me. After taking my daughter, my money and leaving me high and dry, I was suddenly pressed to see how she planned to remedy that.

Sighing, the tears slowly began to escape her eyes as she continued. "Anyway, I was unhappy for a long time before I finally decided to move on, Chez. Not only was I lonely, but I knew all about the women who took up all your time." Wiping tears from her face, she said, "You were supposed to belong to me, and somewhere along the way you forgot that. I tried to be the best woman I could be to you, but I found that my best just wasn't good enough. Then, I received a call from a young lady named Neeta one day, and she told me everything about the two of you. I can't lie, my whole world collapsed at that point…"

Thinking to myself that all her words up to this point were official, I was still waiting for the portion of her story where she would tell me how she planned to make shit right.

"It was then that I met Supreme…" She paused to wipe her eyes once more, and exhaled. "He made it easy for me to fall victim to what I now know, was nothing more than a game. Supreme gave me all the love, affection and attention I had been lacking in our relationship for so long. Yet, it was years before I found out that the two of you were enemies. Please don't hate me, Chez! Believe me, had I known then what I know now, I would have never done what I did."

I felt where she was coming from. She had been a good woman for years, but as far as I was concerned she was nothing more than another good girl gone bad. I couldn't feel sorry for her when she had repaid herself for any troubles I may have put her through with over 1.5 million dollars of my dough.

Checking the time on my watch, I spoke in a dry tone. "I hear you, ma, but how about you get to the part where you explain to me how you plan to make it right?" Turning my drink up, I had already made up my mind that if she was just wasting my time, I was gonna bounce.

"Supreme has over five million dollars in a safe at our house, and I want you to have it," Monya blurted out, rising up from the couch and leaning towards me.

I had a clear view of her breasts, and her raised skirt gave me a straight shot of her naked, hairy pussy.

"If you want the money, it's yours, Chez," she sincerely exclaimed, and licked her lips seductively.

"Yeah, I want it," I replied as cool and calmly as I possibly could. With such a sum being virtually placed in my hands, calm was the last thing I felt at the moment. Figuring that I'd see exactly how much she really wanted to repay her debt, I stated, "I also want him dead. Can you get me close enough to him to handle that as well, Red?"

Pausing as if she needed to work out a plan in her head, she grabbed my thigh and mumbled, "I'll do whatever you need me to do, Chez."

The dreamy look I saw in her eyes when she locked them with mine said it all. She needed to be fucked, and right now, I was the one for the job. I leaned towards her and covered her mouth with my own. I hungrily began to kiss her. Pulling her dress up around her hips, I tasted the inside of her mouth and felt her shudder as a moan escaped her. I stood and pulled her up from the couch, in the process, breaking our kiss. I turned her around and pressed her shoulders forward so that she knew to bend over.

Breathing heavily, she looked over her shoulder with sex-glazed eyes. "Please fuck me!" she pleaded, spreading her legs and raising her ass higher in the air.

No response was necessary. Dropping my pants and boxers, I positioned my dick between the wet folds of her pussy and slammed my weight into her. The loud cry that erupted from her spurred me on. Violently hitting the pussy, I listened to her whimpering moans with no emotion. Although the pussy was still good, I received no pleasure from the act itself. She meant nothing to me. This fuck was strictly for Supreme and the money.

Chapter 18

Cruising towards 16th Street to link up with Monty, I replayed the scene with Monya over in my head. On the outside, she still resembled the woman I had fallen in love with long ago. Nonetheless, she had changed, and although the change wouldn't be evident to a stranger, her cold heartedness was clear to me. The sad part was, she had only become a product of my example. Supreme had the ultimate snake in his camp, and little did he know that I had his ass right where I wanted him. She was practically gonna lay his head on a platter for me, and give me his dough at the same time. The bitch was definitely cold, but this time it was in my favor, so who was I to complain?

Smiling at the thought that every dog has its day, I surveyed the scene around me as I rode through Monty's block. They had a serious setup going on, and the money that came through their strip was ridiculous to say the least. Upon entering their block, on either side of the street, niggas sat on porches, faking nods. They held big pillows in each of their laps. Beneath the pillows, each of the unsuspecting lookouts cradled AR-15 assault rifles. Other spots around the block boasted the same security. Thus, it was known by thieves, snitches and stickup men alike, that 16th Street wasn't having it.

Spotting Monty up ahead standing beside his Lexus with Dozier at his side, I could tell by the array of expensive whips around him, that his crew was out in full force. I needed them, and after tonight, everyone that held me down would be paid well for their contribution.

We had reached the last step in my master plan. Now, the only thing that lay between my repaying Supreme for everything he'd done to me, taking his riches, and living the remainder of my days in the tropics, was Monya. As I pulled up beside Monty, I just hoped that Monya would hold up her end of the bargain. As much as I hated to admit it, I needed her to come through for me.

Monya's body still tingled from the earlier sexcapade with Chez. Even as she moved around the mansion making preparations for his arrival, she continued to relive the episode in her mind. Though she had already planned to clear an easy path for his entrance, and no matter how much scheming was necessary, Supreme's being away from home made the process much easier.

She came across a 9-mm while snooping through Supreme's office. Instead of putting it back where she had found it, Monya decided to keep it. In the event that things got rough, she figured that the weapon would come in handy.

She strolled through the house in deep thought. She was anxious to get the night over with. After she handled this last task, Chez said that they were going somewhere new and exciting. Having him inside her again had been exciting enough. Being wrapped in his arms after so many years had truly been nothing short of a dream. But what had really shocked her was when he began to talk about starting a new life in Jamaica. It was so easy to imagine the feel of the warm sandy white beach beneath her bare feet as she walked hand in hand with him.

Pushing the hidden panel in the wall, it registered in her mind that she couldn't wait to make her escape from Supreme and the many haunting memories that plagued their lives together. She watched as the panel opened to expose a long corridor. She realized that many of the horrors she had experienced would never be spoken of. She closed the panel behind her and headed down the hall. She decided that they would just die along with the man who had put her through them.

Monya reached a flight of stairs and descended them, following the path that Supreme had shown her years before. No one besides the two of them even knew of the escape route's existence. To make sure that it remained a secret, he had gone as far as having everyone who helped build it murdered.

Only feet away from the exit, Monya couldn't help the shudder that passed through her at the thought of just how cruel Supreme had become through the years. It was only the realization that it would all end tonight that spurred her on. The freedom that lay ahead was a more than welcome thought.

Unlocking the bolt from the inside, Monya stepped outside into the cool evening air. Looking around her, she quickly noticed that the sun was slowly beginning to set, which meant that the time was nearly upon her. The coming darkness would not only bring death, it would give her back the life she had waited for what seemed like an eternity for.

Realizing that she needed to be getting back to the house before Supreme arrived, she left the door ajar for Chez, and quickly made her way back. It wouldn't do for Supreme to catch wind of her plot. Not only would he kill her, the army of security who patrolled their estate would slaughter Chez when he arrived. Making a mental note to call and inform Chez about the increase in security, she safely entered the house and closed the panel behind her. Breathing heavily as she strained her ears for any sounds that would alert her to Supreme's return, she sighed in relief once she concluded that he wasn't there.

She hurried out of the room to call Chez. Monya hoped that he would hold up his end of the bargain, because hers had been completed. The ball was now in his court.

On the short ride from the main gate to the house, Supreme silently surveyed the grounds around the estate. Through his close observation, he was able to see that like Mann had reported, security was super tight.

Meeting the Bentley as it came to a stop in front of the house,

Mann opened the door for Supreme to exit. Two members of their crew surrounded them with AK 47's in hand, and man eating Rottweilers that stood at the ready.

Reaching out to grasp his cousin's shoulder in greeting, Mann stated, "With the strength we've built up around here, it will take an army to infiltrate this place."

Supreme gave his cousin a pound in response to his statement as they headed towards the house. Like Mann, he too was aware that no one would be able to get him here. Mann had done a good job, and thanks to him, the estate now resembled a fortress.

Heading up the stairs that led to the house, Supreme sternly stared at the huge columns that lined the archway. It never ceased to amaze him just how far he'd come in life. Unlike the drug-ridden, rat infested projects he had come from, the mini-mansion that loomed ahead of him was magnificent. There was no doubt that he had done well for himself, and now that he had achieved the riches that others only dreamed of, there was no way that he would allow anyone to ruin what he had worked for.

"I've got the whole city on alert for Chez too, cuz," Mann commented, snapping Supreme from his thoughts. "With a million dollar reward riding on his head, I'm sure that we should have him where we want him, real soon."

Supreme's stern look immediately turned cold at the mention of Chez. If he had never hated anyone in life, he truly hated Chez. From the beginning, Chez had been a thorn in his side. Not only had he orchestrated multiple robberies for large sums of money and product, he had murdered numerous members of their crew. That was more than enough reason for his hatred. But it was neither the money nor the product that really counted. Even the members of their crew who fell at Chez's hand weren't the reason. The way he had executed Rio, then tortured Unique in such an inhuman fashion was what fueled Supreme's hatred.

Entering the house followed by Mann, Supreme's mind raced in many directions all at once. Suddenly feeling overwhelmed with all the tasks that needed his attention, he concluded that nothing would be handled until his archenemy had been captured and dealt with. The last time he had escaped with his life, but Supreme made a silent oath to himself that the next time they met would be different. Chez would die, and that was all there was to it.

Between reading a novel and daydreaming about the child she carried and the future that awaited her and Chez, Toshia found herself in a restless state. The sound of the ringing phone snapped her out of her dream state, causing her to scurry out of bed in her haste to reach it. She grabbed the phone and breathlessly spoke into the receiver. "Hello."

"How's my baby girl doing?"

The voice that greeted her, immediately brought a smile to her face. "I'm fine," she excitedly responded. "I must have willed you to call, because I was just thinking about you, baby."

"Oh, you were, huh?" Chez laughed. "Well, I was thinking about you too, ma. You know I miss you, right?"

"Of course I do!" Toshia replied, cradling the phone tightly against her ear as she climbed back in bed. Savoring the sweet sound of Chez's voice, she giggled. "I miss you more! Now, when are you coming home?"

"Sooner than you realize," he stated matter-of-factly. "By later on tonight, or no later than tomorrow, I'll be there with you, baby."

"You mean it's actually going to be over?" she exclaimed excitedly. Wanting him to return home safe and sound, she spoke in a serious, passionate voice. "Please be careful, Chez! I need you here with me, and I don't want anything to keep you from making it to where you belong. Now, do I make myself clear?"

"Yeah, I think you made yourself real clear," Chez replied with a serious tone that matched hers. "It will definitely be over tonight, and nothing will interfere with me making it home. Believe that! Look, ma, I've got to go, but start packing everything up. Tomorrow we're out of here. I love you, girl!"

Before she could respond, the call ended. Toshia could only listen to the dial tone as she cradled the phone to her ear. Unable to release the receiver, she couldn't control the sudden sadness that overwhelmed her at the thought that things may not turn out as well as she hoped. She truly loved Chez with all her heart and soul. Now, she just hoped that her sixth sense wasn't correct for once.

Ending the call with Toshia, I couldn't help the sigh that unconsciously escaped my parted lips. I missed her, and even though I realized that after this was done, we would live happily ever after, I wanted to be there with my boo, now. She was the one woman that I knew I could build my dream life with. If it was my destiny, a dream life was exactly what we would be embarking on in the next 24-hours.

Thinking of Mia and the warning she had given, hit me like a ton of bricks. I was tired of the bloodshed and vengeance I'd been consumed with since returning home. Somewhere along the way, I had lost my bloodlust, and the whole revenge scheme no longer seemed as interesting to me as it once did. For the first time ever, I was filled with doubt, and it was eating at me.

Was it truly my destiny to kill Supreme and take his money? Or was I possibly detouring from my prearranged path? I was already paid, therefore, what was to stop me from cutting my losses and heeding Mia's warning? The exotic beach, drinks that sported fancy umbrellas, and smooth reggae grooves awaited me. I had no answers to any of the questions that plagued me, and even if I did, it was too late to worry about it.

Riding slowly past the sprawling estate, I looked on it in silent contemplation. Other than the breathing of the occupants who surrounded me, the Comp Cable van we rode in was quiet. Each of the men within were lost in their own thoughts. This was expected, due to none of us knowing what the outcome of our mission would be. If we survived, this would serve to be the day that our lives changed for the better. If we failed, it would only be the end of our life long stride towards a come up.

In deep thought, I glared at the expanse of the house and huge grounds that sat on the other side of the fence. Set in the fashion of an 18th century plantation home, but with more of a modern flare, I grudgingly admitted that Supreme had good taste. The mansion was surrounded by a fence that I gauged to be no less than 15 feet tall. Security patrols could be seen within, walking deadly looking Rottweilers with assault rifles slung over their shoulders. I couldn't help the indecision that slowly began creeping its way into my subconscious at the task before me. Why was I doing this? Unlike the men with me, things were no longer dire to the point of jeopardizing my life. I had the woman who had lovingly held me down throughout my otherwise lonely bid, and millions of dollars stacked away. Second guessing my motives, I truly questioned whether the revenge I now sought was even justified at this point.

"Yo, Chez, is that their crib?" Monty asked, with his eyes locked on the passing mansion.

"Umm hmm." I replied, thinking that at this point, there would be no turning back. The rapid sounds of clips being popped in assault rifles all around me sealed the deal. There was no doubt in my mind that Monty and the hand-picked members of his crew were ready for war.

Reluctant, but past the point of return, I followed the directions I'd been given earlier. I pulled into the driveway of the vacant mansion that sat two properties down from Supreme's and I drove around to the back of the dark house. Coming to a stop, I was immediately able to spot the shed-like structure I was told would house the tunnel.

I swiveled in my seat to face Monty. Locking eyes, I blurted out, "You ready, nigga?"

With burning embers shooting from his eyes, his reply was high pitched and straight to the point when he said, "Hell yeah!"

Removing his fiery eyes from me, he returned his focus back to the task he was working on. Cradling the deadly SK assault rifle on his lap, Monty effortlessly began to screw on a muffler attachment that I had never seen before. The silencer would turn the already deadly weapon into a silent weapon of death.

I exited the van, and wasn't surprised to find that the other members of the crew carried the muffler attachments on the tips of their weapons as well. Strapping on my bulletproof vest, Monty handed me one of the modified weapons to go along with the .357 magnum with infrared scope I already carried. Giving him a pound, I hesitantly stated, "Let's handle our business, Lil Bro."

"Let's do it then!" he responded, waving his crew on.

As we made our way towards the shed and tunnel within, it hit me that he was my only friend. Other than my daughter and Toshia, Monty was more or less the only family I had left. Entering the tunnel, I hit the flashlight to illuminate our path.

For some odd reason, as soon as the tunnel lit up, old thoughts of past friends seemed to come to me. With every step I took, another ghost from my past would glare at me in silent disgust. The faces of the many people who had shared my path through the years were as clear to me as if they still lived and breathed.

I shut my eyes tightly to block out the visions as I continued along the path I'd set for myself. It was unknown to me what waited at the other end of the long dark tunnel, but what I did know, was that whatever my destiny called for, I would be prepared for it.

I snapped out of my thoughts as we arrived at our destination. In the next few minutes, I would be inside the mansion that held Supreme and his riches.

Chapter 19

Nervously glancing at her watch every few minutes, Monya chewed on her nails as she paced back and forth through the room. She whispered under her breath, "Where the hell are you, Chez?"

She couldn't figure out what the holdup was. He needed to hurry, because Supreme seemed suspicious of her. Maybe she was experiencing a guilty conscience, but the look he tossed her way each time he passed, just seemed somewhat unusual. This, combined with her anxiety, had the effect of making her extremely uncomfortable.

She shook the thought off to the best of her ability. Monya concluded that she was experiencing nothing more than cold feet. Only, with the scheme already in motion, it was too late for her to have a change of heart.

Hearing approaching footsteps from the direction of the hidden passageway, she hurriedly moved towards the wall to open the locked panel. Unsnapping the safety, she stood to the side and allowed the wall to slide open, giving Chez access into the room. The nervous excitement she experienced at the sight of him, followed by a group of individuals she had never laid eyes on before, was like no other feeling she had ever felt. Staring through unblinking eyes, the sound of Chez's voice slowly snapped her out of her trance-like state.

"Monya!" Chez called out. "Monya! Where is Supreme?"

"In his office," Monya mumbled, somewhat taken aback at the cold manner in which Chez addressed her. Suddenly alarmed, but not sure why, she cut her eyes in the direction of the treacherous looking strangers and thought that for some reason, Chez seemed distant.

"Where is the money?" he asked, cutting into her thoughts. He fired off series of questions at her before she could even answer the first one. "How many men does he have in the house, and did you get my daughter out of here like I told you?"

"Uh… the safe and money are in his office, and Mann is the only one in the house with him. The rest of them are outside. Chanae is safe and sound at Grandmother's house…" Monya's voice trailed off.

Hearing that Mann was in the house along with Supreme, I grinned deviously, thinking that I couldn't possibly be lucky enough to catch the two of them together. They had an opposing force outside, but I knew that they weren't prepared for anyone to creep past their security and actually make it to them. I had already succeeded in doing the unexpected. Now, I was ready to end their lives, take Supreme's riches, and escape unscathed. We had the element of surprise in our favor, and I planned to keep it that way. The faster we handled our task, the better our chances were of not having to shoot it out with security.

Wasting no time, I blurted, "Monya, lead the way to Supreme's office." I then turned to face my crew, and stated, "Let's make this quick, so we can all leave in one piece."

We followed Monya out of the room and down a winding staircase, I couldn't seem to shake off a feeling of impending doom. Grasping my weapon tighter, I was aware that anything could happen from this point on. But, as I quickened my pace, I concluded that there would be no turning back, regardless of the outcome.

"Yeah, nigga, that's how you do it!" Mann barked excitedly, watching Nas and DMX pull off their stickup scene in Belly.

Sipping a glass of Remy Martin while sitting behind a huge white oak desk with his gator booted feet resting on top, Supreme peered at the 80-inch screen with unseeing eyes. His mind was far removed from the movie or anything that was taking place around him.

"Cuz, did you peep that shit?" Mann asked, getting Supreme's attention. "Them motherfuckers put their gangster down like us!" he remarked with a chuckle.

"Whatever!" Supreme countered with a groan. Draining his drink, he added, "It's easy to play a gangster in the movies, nigga! Living this shit ain't the same, and you better not forget it!"

Shooting Supreme an evil stare, Mann took a hit of the blunt he held and shook his head. His cousin was on some other shit lately, and Mann wasn't with it. Turning his attention back to the movie, he decided that once the situation with Chez was cleared up, he was going to call it quits. He had more than enough money to start fresh, anywhere he chose. Plus, with the way Supreme was recklessly running around like he owned the city, it was only a matter of time before the feds arrived. He had experienced more than enough penitentiaries in his time, and the thought of doing life was far from an inviting prospect.

Seeing that the screen went blank, he jerked his head in Supreme's direction and angrily blurted out, "What the hell is your problem?"

"You're my problem!" Supreme spat, tossing the remote on the desk. "Look at yourself!" he barked angrily. "We've got a major problem running rampant in the streets, doing God knows what to our people and business, and you're relaxing around here, bragging on some fake ass niggas in a movie!"

"What?" Mann blared with fire in his eyes. "Who the hell are you to be sweating me about anything? For years, all you've been doing is running around like you're the king of the city, while I do all the dirty work!" Rambling on, Mann was unable to think straight in his rapidly increasing anger. "Mann, do this… Mann, do that! If it wasn't for me, you would never have been in Virginia in the first place, nigga! But maybe like everything else you seem to have forgotten, you don't remember that either, huh?" he taunted, tossing Supreme a patronizing smirk.

"So, that's how you feel, huh, cuz?" Supreme laughed as their eyes locked in a silent battle. "If it wasn't for you, none of this shit would have been possible, huh?" he asked in a mocking tone. Before Mann could answer, he shouted, "Fuck that, and fuck you, nigga!"

"That's the same way I feel about you!" Mann yelled, preparing to stand.

Slowly inching his hand towards the gun he kept hidden under the desk, Supreme's mind was blank as he stared at Mann. Cousin or not, he had already decided that if Mann stood up, he would murder him. The way he saw it, disrespect from anyone was unacceptable, and the inferno in his eyes should have warned Mann of his intentions.

Mann had just reached a standing position when the loud booming sound of the office door crashing inward snapped him out of the staring match he and Supreme were locked in. Too stunned to react, both of their eyes widened at the realization that they weren't as untouchable as they had thought they were.

Quickly entering the room followed by Monty, Chez caught Mann square in the face with the butt of an SK. The force of the blow split open his forehead and sent him falling face-first to the carpet. Chez walked straight towards Supreme who sat with an expressionless look on his face, as Monty disarmed Mann.

Locking his gaze on Chez and the others who had just barged into his office, Supreme couldn't believe what he was seeing. The only thought that ran through his mind was, How did they get past my security?

It was then that he saw Monya enter the room with a smug, contempt-filled look that was directed at him. Seething inside at the knowledge of her deceit, he forgot about the many weapons that were aimed in his direction and threatened, "Bitch, you're gonna suffer the slowest, most vicious death, ever when I get my hands on you!"

"You ain't killing shit!" Chez cut in with a sinister smile. "You're the one who's about to die slow, nigga!"

Seeing the evil grimace that stretched across his features, I decided to taunt him a little longer before actually killing him. I pointed the SK at his chest. "Ain't it crazy how shit changes? The last time we met like this, it was you who held the gun." Cutting my eyes at Monya, I sharply stated, "We don't got all day, ma. Get my money while I finish this clown's ass off!"

Watching Supreme's head jerk in Monya's direction as she hurriedly ran to do my bidding, I couldn't help repeating the words he had said to me before he left me in a puddle of blood to die. "I'll be sure to take care of your bitch for you, nigga!"

Before I could squeeze the trigger, Supreme surprised me by screaming, "Fuck that bitch! Die, nigga!"

He lunged across the desk with a 9-mm in his hand.

Caught off guard by the numerous bullets that slammed into his face and upper torso, I stood rooted to my spot, somewhat baffled by what had just taken place. Slumped over the desk with his brains leaking out of the side of his head, Supreme stared back at me with wide, unseeing eyes.

Barking dogs and loud knocking outside snapped me out of my daze. Turning around, I had to do a double take when I spotted Monya standing behind me with her weapon still aimed in Supreme's direction. I shook my head at the irony of the whole situation. I couldn't believe that she had actually killed him.

Although her quick trigger skills had saved my life, we no longer had the element of surprise at our disposal. The gunshots had alerted the security of our presence, and suddenly it didn't seem like we would be leaving without a fight after all.

Regaining control of myself and the situation, I began to calmly give orders. "Get the safe open and put that damn pistol away." Pausing to watch Monya scurry behind Supreme's desk, I turned to face Monty. "Lil' brah, put half of our crew in the front hallway just in case those fools outside roll up in here. We'll use the rest of them to pack the money up."

Hearing Mann moan as he slowly began to regain consciousness, I lifted the SK, aimed it down onto his outstretched frame and released a short burst into his jerking body.

I cracked a smile. It was finally over, and the two men that I hated the most in the world no longer existed.

"Oh, shit!" I stated to no one in particular, at the movement I felt beneath my feet. Whatever Monya had done when she went behind Supremes desk caused the carpet to retract, uncovering a huge floor safe. Between the hidden passageway and the electrical carpet, it was apparent that the nigga had been on some "James Bond" shit. After today, it was clear to me that I hadn't seen it all, after all.

Rushing from behind the desk at the sound of weapons being fired, Monya dropped to her knees and quickly began to turn the combination dial as if she had done it many times before.

Hearing the clicking sound that signified the sequence of numbers were correct, she stood and moved to the side. "It's all yours," she informed me, smiling nervously.

I moved past her, and reached for the handle and yanked the heavy door open. What I saw when I peered into the vast chamber was unbelievable. Blinking to make sure that my eyes weren't deceiving me, I turned and stared at Monya.

"What?" she asked in a worried tone while hugging herself. "What's wrong, baby?"

"I don't know who the hell told you there was five million dollars in here..."

"I swear, the money was there, Chez! I would never lie about something like that--"

Cutting her words short, I blurted out, "There has to be at least ten million dollars up in this bitch!"

Hearing her intake of breath and sudden silence, it was clear that my words had caught her completely off guard as well. The rows of individually wrapped, white brick-shaped packages alone had to be worth another ten million dollars at least.

Yelling over the loud gunfire, I summoned Monty.

"Yeah, yeah! What's all the screaming about?" he asked, entering the room followed by Lavar and E.J. He glanced into the cavernous safe. His eyes widened, and he came to an abrupt halt.

Gauging his reaction, it was clear that I wasn't alone in my shock. But now wasn't the time to choke up. We had a mission to complete, and from the sounds of the battle that was raging outside, we were on borrowed time.

"Grab those duffel bags and let's get this shit packed up. We need to be out of here ASAP!" I emphasized in a firm tone. Snatching one of the bags up myself, I headed down into the vault. I had a mission to complete, and time was one thing that I didn't have a lot of.

Moving as fast as possible, we were able to remove everything from the vault, with the exception of about two million dollars that I left behind for my own reasons.

I tossed Lavar the last duffel bag to take back through the tunnel, and instructed Monty to call the crew off. By the time they returned, I figured that my business with Monya would be concluded, and this chapter of my life would be over with as well.

"We did it!" Monya yelled, throwing her arms around my neck. Pulling away, she excitedly gasped, "I can't wait until we reach Jamaica, baby!"

Staring at her with an ice grill, I cut in before she could continue. "We who? You're not going to Jamaica!" Watching the smile melt from her features, I added, "At least you're not going with me."

"Huh?" she mumbled, not quite getting the message. "What are you talking about? You said that after tonight, we were going to Jamaica to begin our new life, Chez." She shook her head in despair. She couldn't see straight, due to the tears that clouded her eyes.

"Please!" I said, laughing. "Why would I want to start a new life with your trifling ass? Sure, I'm going to begin again in Jamaica. And you want to know something, bitch? I'm in love with someone else, and it's all about her, now. No better yet, how about, I need some time to do me? Isn't that what you told me, Monya? So how does it feel?" I asked. I chuckled in a mocking fashion. "So, this is where we part company, Red. Have a good life, ma!"

Waving to add fuel to the fire, I turned and began to stroll out of the room. I had dreamed about this feeling all the years in prison and I must admit it felt just as good as the dream.

"You can't do this to me! I have nothing left!" Monya screamed at my departing back as the realization set in, that after what she had done to Supreme, I was abandoning her. "Wait!" she pleaded as the tears poured uncontrollably.

I tossed the words over my shoulder. "I left your grimy ass over two million in the safe, which is more than you did for me, so you're good!" I chuckled before adding, "Respect the game and do you!"

I had somewhere to be, and I really wasn't trying to hear anything else she had to say. Plus, I knew that she was straight with over two million to keep her living in the manner she had become accustomed to.

The familiar clicking sound that reached my ears stopped me dead in my tracks. Looking over my shoulder, I nonchalantly stated, "I know you ain't lost your motherfucking mind!"

As if my words had no effect on her, Monya stood with a 9-mm in her hand and a tide of tears pouring down her face. Half-hysterical, her voice cracked as she babbled in a low tone, "You can't do this to me, Chez! I've given up everything for you!" Pointing the gun with shaking hands, in a frenzy, she began to laugh in a psychotic manner and yelled, "I love you, Chez! And if I can't have you, no one will!"

I stared at her without blinking. It was apparent that she wasn't playing any games. I still had the SK in my hand, but the last thing I wanted to do was kill her.

I decided to try reasoning with her. "Monya, put the gun down and let's talk about it."

Rapidly shaking her head from side to side as tears poured uncontrollably, she snickered. "I can't do that, Chez! You... will... only leave me. I'm not gonna let you leave me!" she informed, wiping a long wisp of hair out of her eyes.

I was tired of playing games, and the last thing I planned on doing was hanging around here with her psycho ass. Banking on the fact that she was only bluffing, I shrugged my shoulders and said, "If shooting me is what you plan on doing, then that's what you're gonna have to do. I'm out, ma." I turned around, and without another glance in her direction, I headed for the door. I knew Monya better than I knew myself. Therefore, I knew she wouldn't shoot me.

"Stop, Chez! Don't walk away from me!" she shouted. "I'll shoot! I swear I will!" she warned in a loud, threatening tone.

Blocking out her ranting, I continued walking with thoughts of the trouble free life that awaited Toshia and I. I'd been through so much, and it was finally over. My come up was complete, and the time had arrived to enjoy the fruits of my labor.

In a bone chilling voice, Monya screamed, "We'll always be together, motherfucker!"

Then, she pulled the trigger.

"Boom! Boom! Boom!" were the deafening sounds Monty heard as he returned to notify Chez that they were all set to go. Running towards the office with his weapon primed and ready, the sight that greeted him was beyond his comprehension.

Lying in a flowing puddle of blood by the door, Chez's was face down on the floor.

Monty was only a millisecond away from firing his SK into the kneeling form of the intruder when he froze. Staring back at him with a wide grin on her angelic face, Monya held the barrel of the 9-mm to her temple.

"I told you not to leave me!" she whispered over and over.

Monty was about to take her out of her misery, but Monya beat him to it. With her hand shivering, she cock back the hammer of the gun, and with one quick motion, pulled the trigger. The bullet entered her head, killing her instantly. Her beautiful body dropped to the floor, like a sack of potatoes.

Monty lowered his weapon and slowly walked past her. As he was about to enter the hallway, he was surprised to hear a cough and gasping for air coming from his friend. Monty quickly turned Chez over to make sure his ears hadn't deceived him. The look on his friend's face showed that he was in extreme pain, but was definitely still alive.

"What the fuck happened!" Monty screamed with joy in his voice

"I... didn't... think the... bitch had it in her," I responded, still gasping for air.

The force of the bullets had my back throbbing like hell, and had knocked the wind out of me. I attempted to take a deep breath and gather my thoughts. Monty grabbed me under my arms and lifted me up into his chest. My head was spinning and I could tell that my equilibrium was off. Monty placed my right arm over his left shoulder, and we began to limp out the room.

It was a good thing I had decided to wear a bulletproof vest, otherwise, Monty would have been walking out of here alone. I thought to myself. I smiled and inwardly thanked God for sending me that angel in the store that day. Her warning had made me take a precaution that I had never done in my life, and it had truly paid off. Outside of the bullet fragment that had torn into my shoulder and caused the rapid amount of blood loss, I was fine.

We quickened our pace, and took the stairs three at a time in our rush to leave the mansion and the carnage inside.

Reaching the tunnel, Monty and I both took one last look into the room before closing the panel and heading through the passageway. Over ten million dollars awaited us, and we were in a hurry to get to it. I would never forget Monya, but my new life was just getting started, and at that moment, that's what mattered most.

I began to grin at the realization of how rich we were as Monty and I exited the passageway.

Even though my back ached, my shoulder throbbed from the gunshot wound, and my head was pounding like a drum, there was only one thought on my mind.

Damn, this game is deeper than love.

Please Be Sure To Check Out These Other Titles From Blake Karrington As Well.

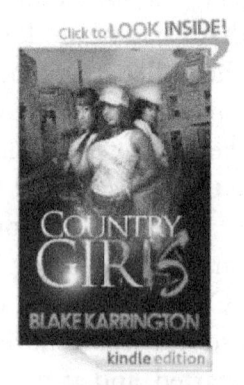

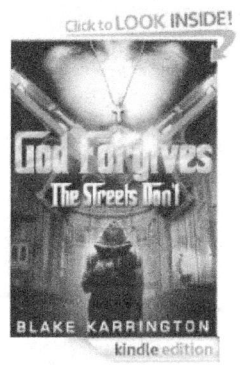

@BlakeKarrington
Blake Karrington

Made in the USA
Monee, IL
13 March 2024